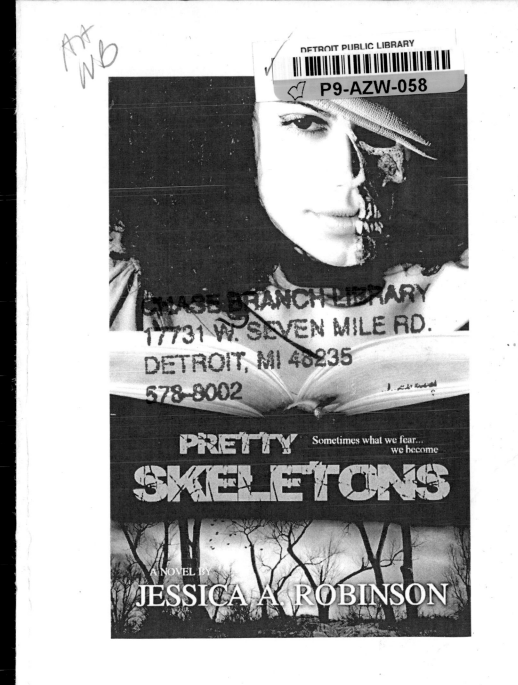

**PRETTY**

Sometimes what we fear...
we become

# SKELETONS

A NOVEL BY

## JESSICA A. ROBINSON

JUN 10

Giving Your Soul a Rise...One Page at a Time

Peace In The Storm Publishing, LLC.
P.O. Box 1152
Pocono Summit, PA 18346

Visit our Web site at www.PeaceInTheStormPublishing.com

Literary Awards Show

Peace In The Storm Publishing, LLC is the winner of the
2009 African American Literary Award for
Independent Publisher of the Year.

# pretty skeletons

A NOVEL BY JESSICA A. ROBINSON

Peace In The Storm Publishing, LLC

# author's note

I was about halfway done with completing this novel when a virus attacked my computer files and completely erased my entire book! I was devastated and hurt because I had worked very hard so, for it to be all gone, made me feel like it was all done for nothing. But, in the middle of that, I came to a sense of peace and prayed about it then God reminded me of a place where I had a portion of the story so all wasn't lost.

I learned a valuable lesson. I will always make sure I save everything to my external hard drive however, more valuable than that, I realized you may face setbacks and roadblocks in your way when you're trying to do something but it's not a indication that you need to give up. Instead, it suggests you are in the right place at the right time and that's the strength you need to keep on going. So, if you're facing a struggle in your life, be encouraged. God will give you the wisdom and instruction on how to proceed. The most important thing for you to do is keep moving forward.

God Bless,

_Jessica_

# acknowledgements

I would like to thank my Lord and Savior Jesus Christ for making this dream of mine possible. Even when I think that I don't deserve to be blessed, you do something else to let me know you're still in the blessing business. Thank you from the bottom of my heart for this gift.

To my Gabe and Mike, thank you for being so wonderful to me, for dropping what you're doing to come with me when it's time to get on the road and travel. I'm so grateful to have you two in my life.

To my Grandpa Nate, Grandma Ruth, and Grandpa Willard, I really love you guys.

I'm also thankful to Brandon, Sean, and Jason for being brothers to me as well. You guys are great! Backdraft Ent., let's get 'em! Yall really aren't ready! www.carnivalhhh.com and check it out for yourself!

Shannon, Lillie, and Monica, it goes without saying but you are my sisters. I love you.

To the Robinson, Oliver, Weaver, Rowe, Wright, Rios, Peterman, and Brown families, I love you all. Thank you for being who you are. I'm blessed to have you as my family.

To Mother Wright, Tiki, and Aunt Carol... simply I love you. Aunt Carol thanks for cheering me on and, Mother Wright, the sequel to "Holy Seduction" is coming soon. Hold on! Lol

To Diane Martin, Fred Martin, Greg, Amy, and Carrie, thanks for being there for me. I love you all and, even though we don't see enough of each other, we're still family.

Valerie aka "Miss V," you have definitely been a lifesaver during the course of this book. Thanks for all your help and having fast typing skills!

Tiffany "T-Luv" Allen, thank you for not only helping to promote me and my stories but also for being a special friend to me.

To Happy Monroe, thanks for being the first person to officially read "Pretty Skeletons." I appreciate you from the bottom of my heart.

Thanks to NaTasha Gooch, Sarah Hooker, Zulema Hooker, Jen Lynch, Kendrail Banks, Leslie Wright, Shasta Shabazz, Maurice Gooch, Devan Franklin, Latoya Simmons, Joi Pagan, and Claude "Deuce" Harris Jr. Thanks for being my friends. Everyone in their own way hold special places in my heart.

Sarah Brown, thanks for all your support to me and granting me one of my first interviews for "Holy Seduction."

Thank you to Amanda Rodriguez, Cynthia Torres, Marsha Geer, and Brian Hunt for being such cool co-workers.

To Trice Hickman, thanks for the amazing friendship we have. I appreciate how much help and advice you've provided over this past year to me. I pray that God continues to bless you in all you do.

To Crystal and Stacia, thank you for not only being my cousins but you are truly my sisters. I love you.

Special thanks to Ms. Candy for the awesome job you did for the Holy Seduction book launch party. I really appreciate it.

To Venesha Hope, thanks for all your advice and expertise. You're such a wonderful person and friend.

To Mari Walker, Suzetta Perkins, Tamika Newhouse, Monda Webb, Ni'Cola Mitchell, Ndea B., Nikkea Smithers, Frankie Nicole, Renee Flagler, Kimani Nelson, V.J. Gotastory, Angel Mechelle, K.D. Harris, James Jimason, Linda Herman, Tinisha N. Johnson, Theresa Gonsalves, D.L. Sparks and Tina McKinney, thank you for inspiring me to keep going on. I've learned a lot and I'm glad to have come into contact with you all.

Thanks to Tra Verdejo and T. Styles for the wonderful book signings while in the DMV area. If you're in the area, please make sure you stop by Tra's bookstand in Patapsco Flea Market in Baltimore and T. Styles bookstore, Cartel Café and Books in Oxon Hills, MD... Absolutely beautiful! Thanks to Marcus Williams and Nubian Bookstore in Morrow, Ga for a great signing as well.

Special thanks to Davida Baldwin for the smoking hot cover she designed for "Pretty Skeletons." This is why you're the coldest, most talented graphic designer in the land! Don't believe me? Go to www.oddballdsgn.com and see for yourself.

To my fabulous all-star editor Rhonda Crowder, thanks for being there with me through this entire process and challenging my growth as a writer. Thanks for also being my friend. If you're in need of superb editing services, contact her at paydapiper@aol.com. Special thanks to LoVetta and Wayne of 31TenMagazine. I appreciate all the support you've shown me.

Thanks to Expressions Book Club, RWA Book Club, AAMBC, Sistah Confessions Book Club, Hot Topix Book Club, Royal Readers Book Club, Sweet Soul Sisters and Literary Divas Book Club for supporting "Holy Seduction." I truly appreciate it! Also, I would like to thank Rhonda Bogan and D'On Ingram of Mocha Readers for the wonderful event "Authors on the Yard" at Central State University.

I would like to thank Linda Pate and Precious Memories Bookstore for all their support. Thanks for the review you wrote in your "Urban Views Weekly" column.

A special thanks to my readers, new and old. I thank you for choosing to support me. I continue to write more stories because of you. I also learn more because of you too. Thanks and continue to spread the word!

Last, but definitely not least, a very special thank you to my publisher Elissa Gabrielle. Thanks for taking a chance on me and for believing in me. I promise I won't disappoint you. You're a wonderful woman and you are truly a person of integrity. If you haven't already please visit, www.peaceinthestormpublishing.com to purchase some really great reads.

If you would like to contact me or find out more about my work and upcoming events, please feel free to check out, www.jessica-robinson.com, www.carnivalhhh.com, www.twitter.com/holyseduction, www.facebook.com/jessicaarobinson, www.myspace.com/holyseductionthenovel, and my email address songbird352000@yahoo.com

God Bless,

Jessica A. Robinson

# Dedication

I dedicate my novel to two special people. First, I would like to dedicate this story to my grandma Margaret Ann. You always encouraged me to pursue my dream no matter what and you read everything I wrote. Even if it made no sense, you still deemed it a strike of genius. I love you and can't wait to see you again. Kiss mommy and daddy for me.

I dedicate my novel to my godson Terrence "T.J." Tarver. You were my little angel and even though I feel you left us too soon I know God doesn't make any mistakes. You will always have a special place in my heart. I love you and know that you are in good hands.

"History always has a way of repeating itself."

-Anonymous-

# prologue (1992)

When Keisha got off the school bus and headed toward the apartment building she called home, she grew excited to see her mom's 1982 white Buick Regal parked outside in the parking lot. She didn't expect her mother to be home but was thankful nonetheless. She walked through the main door to the building, which was already open, and started to make her way up to the fourth floor. She hated how some residents always left the door open because their building stayed infested with all kinds of insects, not to mention small cats and dogs brave enough to venture inside. Keisha was almost afraid to see what kinds of rodents may be roaming around the place she called home.

The wind started to blow outside and managed to push its way past the front door, causing it to fly open. The smell of urine, coupled with weed smoke and pure funk, produced a certain mustiness that threatened to turn Keisha's stomach every time she entered the building. She couldn't stand the fact she lived in such a place with her older brother, younger sister, and her mother. Her mom told them they wouldn't stay there for long. She had to move them into a cheaper place on the lower Eastside of Youngstown in order to save up some money so she could buy a house. She promised to move up out of the low-income housing unit as soon as possible and Keisha continually held on to it. What was supposed to only be a four month stay somehow turned into three and a half years. Even though it didn't seem like they were going to move anywhere, Keisha held onto the promise that her mother made her.

Keisha knocked on the door of their two bedroom apartment, expecting to see her mother Rita answer the door wearing her work clothes. Instead, she saw her brother Alonzo in his Burger King uniform.

"Keisha, why you bangin' on the door like you crazy? You need to chill," he said as he opened up the door wide enough to let her in.

"I'm sorry Alonzo. I thought Ma was home. Her car is outside."

"Yeah that's her car but she ain't home. I don't know where she is. I just came home myself and I have to go to work." Keisha looked up at his name tag that read Alonzo Stewart and always wondered why her last name and Kennedi's last name were different than his but their mother said that was because he took on his father's last name. Keisha's mother told her that she wanted her to have her last name which made her last name Sheridan instead of Stewart like her brother.

Keisha walked pass where Alonzo stood in the kitchen and set her book bag down on the table and noticed there was a note her mother seem to have scribbled down in a hurry. She could barely read the handwriting on the white piece of notebook paper but had taught herself to decipher her mother's words.

*Keisha,*

*I ran out with your Aunt Bunchie and Aunt Shay. I will be back after while. Make sure you stay in the house. I'll be home soon.*

*Love ya baby girl,*
*Ma*

Yeah right, Keisha thought while sucking her teeth and rolling her eyes as she balled up the piece of paper. She couldn't understand for the life of her why her mother insisted on calling Bunchie and Shay her aunts when she knew good and well they were of no relation at all. In fact, Keisha didn't even know where her mother met these two women because they seemed to have appeared in their life out of nowhere. Rita insisted they were both good friends from back in the day when they were all younger but Keisha could never seem to remember their entrance into their lives at all. Instead all she could recall is how much of their mother's time they consumed.

# pretty skeletons

Bunchie and Shay used to portray like they were hardworking women who just wanted to be friends with their mother but Keisha picked up on the fact that they were unemployed and had an affinity for removing items from their apartment when they wanted their "fix." On the surface, they acted like they truly cared for Rita but all they did was use her because, out of the three of them, she was the only one who had a steady job. She was the only one who had a tangible source of income so to drug addicts she was their bread and butter. Keisha may have been a young girl but could see straight through to their true motives.

Rita claimed they were just going out to Choices, the local bar, to have a girl's night out with a couple of drinks but Keisha knew different. She knew a lot went on when they got together. Her so-called aunts swore up and down they were just having some innocent fun when they were out but Keisha knew otherwise. Matter of fact, when Bunchie and Shay were involved, it always equaled trouble. Things in their house came up missing. Rita stayed out later than she was supposed to and, after she came home from partying with them, she never had any money in her wallet.

Even though Keisha was only twelve years old and was naïve by most standards, she knew exactly what her mother did while away from them. Keisha was fully aware that her mother was addicted to crack cocaine. It didn't take a rocket scientist to figure it out and, what she didn't know, she heard from a couple of kids at school who remembered seeing her mother coming out of a few of the crack houses scattered across the city.
At school, she mostly played it off as if the kids who ran up to her telling her these things lied but, deep down inside, she knew it held validity.

Rita had a factory job and made all kinds of money but Keisha, Alonzo, and Kennedi didn't reap much of the benefits. They were forced to walk around with holes in their shoes, old clothes, and it was an absolute miracle if they had food in the house. There were some days that they went without eating because Rita wouldn't come home. However, Alonzo always made sure he did his best to keep everything together. Since he was the eldest of three, he picked up the slack when their mother wasn't around, which meant he had kept a steady job since he was old enough to work. If it wasn't for the money Alonzo brought in, a lot of times they wouldn't have eaten at all. Their mother was even awarded a food stamp card but, most of the time, they never benefited from it because she sold her stamps for more money to get high. Sometimes, Alonzo and Keisha were reduced to stealing their mother's card to buy a few groceries before she gave them all away for her next high.

"Alonzo, please don't go to work today. Stay home with me. We can watch movies. I'll even let you pick it."

"I wish I could Keesh but can't. I gotta go to work."

Keisha knew her brother couldn't afford to miss a day but thought whining a little would lead him to give in just this once. She wished he could call off so they could spend some time together since it seemed like he worked more than their mother. And with him at work or school and Rita at work or getting high, Keisha and Kennedi were often left at home by themselves.

"Okay Alonzo, but bring me home a double cheeseburger 'cuz I'll be hungry."

"Well I can bring you home a sandwich but Ms. Gina said for you and Kennedi to come over and you can have dinner with her and Eric."

"Okay."

"When I get off, if Ma is still not home, then I'll be over to get you two. See you later baby girl." He kissed her on the forehead and was out the door.

Keisha waited for her sister Kennedi to get off the bus. They both went over to Ms. Gina's. Keisha's best friend Eric answered the door and the aroma of red beans and rice filled their nostrils as they walked in. She closed her eyes and took a couple of deep breaths allowing the scent to tickle her taste buds.

"What took you so long to come over?" Eric asked as he shut the door and turned the deadbolt lock.

"I was waiting for my sister to get off the bus."

"Oh, well we were waiting so we can all eat together."

"You didn't have to wait. Kennedi and I would've just had what was left over." "No, we believe in eating together at the same time. We also say grace and before we eat."

"Oh yeah, I forgot about that," Keisha replied as they followed Eric to the table where they all sat down.

She had never heard of anybody saying grace until she started hanging around Eric. He wouldn't even touch a morsel of food without saying a prayer over it. By the time Keisha remembered to pray, she was usually consuming her last bite. She had been raised totally different from Eric but it was their differences that allowed them to become close friends. She honestly didn't even know what praying was until they started eating dinner with them and the first time she'd went to a church service was when she went to a morning service with them. Attending church with them was a different experience for her and was a place she wasn't used to going at all. Her mother didn't even bother to dress them up for Easter or Christmas service. She felt that since she wasn't a regular church member then it wasn't any point in going to those special services just so everyone there would notice that she doesn't go.

"Hello Ms. Keisha and Ms. Kennedi. I'm so glad you ladies made it. We're just about to pray," Ms. Gina announced.

"Okay," Keisha and Kennedi replied in unison.

"Eric, say the grace please." Eric folded his hands, bowed his head, and closed his eyes.

"Lord, please bless the food we're about to receive. In Jesus' name. Amen."

As they sat down at the table, Ms. Gina offered the girls a chance to get their plates first and, like clockwork, Keisha was the first one to take advantage of the offer.

"Keisha, you have to be the greediest girl I know." Eric began to laugh as he saw his friend load up her plate with food. Keisha continued to eat as if she hadn't heard anything he said. She allowed the aroma to infiltrate her senses by traveling through her nostrils. She loved when they were invited over to eat her home cooked meals that appeared as if she was to feed the entire apartment building. She wished her mother would make them dinner at their house and they could sit down and eat together but her mother only cooked for them once in a blue moon when she was in the mood. Her being in the mood to cook didn't seem to be very often but, when her mother received her food stamps every month, they could at least count on one good meal and then it was every man and woman for themselves after that.

"Shut up Eric, you know I love your mother's food."

"So you're still greedy."

"No, I'm not!"

"Ms. Greedy!" Eric laughed as Keisha playfully suckered him in his right arm.

"Cut that out Eric... Keisha can eat whatever she wants."

After they finished eating dinner, Eric wanted her to play Super Mario Brothers on Nintendo with him but Keisha convinced him to watch Video Soul on BET which was one of her favorite shows on television. Kennedi sat close by playing with a few of her Barbie dolls she received the Christmas last year. She wished her sister had new dolls but their mother said they wouldn't be celebrating Christmas that year. Everyone seemed to buy Rita's lie except Keisha because she remembered her mother going shopping for gifts but even those magically disappeared from her mother's bedroom closet. So, instead of telling them the truth, she explained that times were hard and they wouldn't be getting anything for Christmas.

After Video Soul went off, an episode of Martin came on. Just as they were turning the channel to find something else to watch, there was loud knocking at the door. Keisha had automatically thought it was her mother so she woke up her little sister Kennedi and started to collect their things.

When Eric opened up the door, there were two police officers standing there to greet him in full uniform.

"Excuse me, is there an adult home?" the one officer asked as she took out a small notepad and began to write.

"Yes sir, hold on." Eric called out to his mother who was in the kitchen washing dishes. When she reached the door, the officers asked to speak with her in the hallway privately so she walked out, closing the door behind her.

As Ms. Gina stood out there talking to the officers, Keisha and Eric tried to come up with reasons as to why the police were at their front door. After five minutes of brainstorming, they were unable to come up with anything so they went back into the living room and sat down on the couch. The only reason they could figure out that maybe the police were looking for one of their neighbors because they had done something.

Without warning, Gina came back into the apartment and allowed the door to slam behind her which startled Keisha, Eric, and Kennedi, who were all sitting on the couch. The loud sound of the steel door slamming caused them to look directly at Gina who was covered in sweat.

Her tear drenched eyes let Keisha know that something wasn't quite right. Gina sat down in her favorite recliner chair, which sat in the corner of the living room, and looked at Keisha. By the look on her face, Keisha knew whatever she was getting ready say wasn't about to be good news. And from the terrified look on her face, Keisha knew what she was getting ready to say directly pertained to her.

"Keisha, come here baby," she said in between tears.

"Yes ma'am." Keisha walked over to her and grabbed her hand.

"Baby, the police stopped by to tell me that your mom is gone." A whole new stream of tears began to fall down Gina's sandy almond colored skin.

"What? Where did she go?"

"She was out with Bunchie and Shay and she stopped breathing so they called the ambulance but, by the time they got to her, she was already gone."

"So you mean to tell me she's dead?"

Gina nodded her head yes to confirm what Keisha already knew.

"I don't understand what you mean. My mother can't be dead, I just saw her this morning before I left for school!" Keisha proclaimed as tears began to well up in her eyes.

"Honey, I know what I told you doesn't make sense to you but it's true."

Ms. Gina paused before she continued.

Keisha kept blinking her eyes real fast, trying to hold back the tears that had formed. She never expected to hear that type of news. She always thought maybe one day her mom would end up in jail, get beat up, or better yet choose to go to rehab and clean herself up. But she would've never guessed that her mother would be dead.

She shook her head in disbelief, hoping that Ms. Gina would jump in at any moment and inform her that her mother wasn't dead and she would be returning at any moment so they could go home but she never did it.

"Your mother is gone baby."

Upon hearing the conformation that her mother was in fact gone, Keisha lost all control. She kicked and screamed. She threw everything she carried across the room. Ms. Gina didn't stop her from having her tantrum instead she offered her support.

"You do whatever you have to do, Keisha." Gina replied in an effort to console the outraged little girl but Keisha was beyond angry. When she finally exhausted herself, she walked up to Ms. Gina and collapsed into her arms. She held and cried with Keisha as she prayed. She didn't bother to say anything. She didn't bother to say anything back to Ms. Gina. She couldn't because she had absolutely nothing to say. Ms. Gina held and rocked Keisha gently in her arms while she whispered, "Baby girl everything gonna be alright. God's got everything under control."

Ms. Gina was a very religious woman and used to always tell her son Eric and Keisha stories out of the Bible. When she talked, she always mentioned God. Although Keisha had been to church a couple of times, she didn't really know God. But whoever He was, she really hoped He had things under control because in this moment of her young life she felt powerless.

# chapter 1

## December 2008

"Keisha, what brings you in to see me today?" Dr. Karen Stone asked as she sat back in her tan leather office chair and pushed the record button on the tape recorder. Keisha stretched out on the plush brown leather couch and stared up at the ceiling, unsure of where to start. She knew what she wanted to say but all of her thoughts were jumbled in her mind like gumbo. She was unable to collect them to speak. She took a few minutes to get her feel together before she even began to say anything to her therapist.

"It's happening again," Keisha blurted out. Dr. Stone pulled out her yellow legal pad to jot down notes.

"What's happening again? Can you elaborate?" she asked as she paused and observed Keisha's mood.

"The nightmares, cold sweats, the tossing and turning. It's all starting to come back," Keisha replied and closed her eyes.

"How long has this been going on, Keisha?" the doctor pushed her cobalt blue wire framed glasses up on her nose.

"Well, I was fine up until I got a phone call from my aunt Darlene two days ago. Then, things started happening ever since then."

"Okay, so I want you to tell me about this phone call from your aunt."

"I won't answer and I haven't called her back."

"And why haven't you been calling her back?" Dr. Stone asked. Keisha paused a moment trying to search for the right words to provide a sufficient reply to her question. She didn't want to come off as cold and callous but at this point she didn't know any other way to express herself.

"Because, I really don't have a desire to talk to her or Jessie. I know that sounds bad because Darlene is my mother's sister but I really don't have a desire to talk to her. And, I especially don't feel a need to talk to her husband!" Keisha sat up.

"Why don't you want to talk to them? I know during one of our earlier sessions you mentioned the fact they were the only people besides your siblings who were still living, but you don't feel the need to maintain that family connection."

Keisha crossed her arms and directly addressed Karen.

"No because every time they're around me, there's trouble. And just thinkin' about everything I went through as a result keeps me away from them."

"Would you like to expand upon your last statement? What do you mean when you say every time they come around, you experience nothing but trouble? What happened between you and them?" Karen asked as she took a minute to catch up on her notes. She looked up at Keisha who was already shaking her head.

"No offense but I really don't want to get into that right now," Keisha replied and looked off in another direction. Karen put her notepad down on the wooden table next to her chair then pressed the stop button on the tape recorder. She knew the purpose of therapy was to share but she wasn't ready.

"This is the point we always get to and you never want to go past it. I would like you to discuss these things in more detail so I can get a better understanding of what's going on?"

"I'm sorry Karen but I can't. I'm afraid to talk about my past and I'm not comfortable telling you anymore right now. I know I'm here to get help but at least you know where I'm coming from."

"Keisha, I understand where you're coming from and believe me I would never pressure you to share with me until you actually ready to talk about everything, so I'll leave that part up to you and when you're ready. You just let me know."

Keisha got up from the couch and stood on her feet.

"Okay Karen, I wish I could tell when I would be ready to talk about it but the truth is I don't even have a clue."

"Don't worry. No pressure here but please do me a favor."

"What is that?"

"Please promise me you'll pick up the phone if Darlene calls you."

Keisha let out a long sigh and then answered her.

"Okay Karen. I'll try," Keisha promised as she walked out of Karen's office to the receptionist desk where she scheduled her follow-up appointment.

"Mrs. Mahone, when would like your next appointment?" The receptionist asked as she typed something in the computer.

"Wait a second. Let me look at my calendar. I'll let you know." Keisha pulled out her leather checkbook and glanced at her dates. A picture of her family dropped out of the calendar and onto the receptionist desk where she picked it up.

"You have a beautiful family. Are those your kids?" She asked as she pointed to the boy and girl who were smiling from ear to ear in the family portrait.

"Yeah, those are my twins," Keisha smiled.

"How old?"

"Five."

"They're very cute," she replied as she handed the picture back to Keisha. Instead of placing the picture back in her checkbook, she decided to hold it momentarily.

"Oh, I can come next Thursday."

"Same time?"

"That's fine."

The receptionist handed Keisha a white business card with her next appointment written on it and she stuffed it inside her purse. She made sure she dug deep in her purse and placed the card at the bottom to ensure it wouldn't slip out. Keisha didn't want to run the risk of carrying the card in her hand. She was afraid she might leave it somewhere where her husband or children might find it. She didn't want anyone to know she saw a therapist. Keisha was too embarrassed to tell anyone she was seeing a shrink.

As far as she was concerned, people who elected to see a shrink were completely crazy. Or, at least, that's what she was told in the past. But, over the course of a couple weeks, she had endured so much personal torment she came to the conclusion that maybe therapy could do her some good. That's why she looked in the phone book and scheduled an appointment with one who didn't look threatening or too pushy. The minute she came across Dr. Karen's advertisement she determined her to be the obvious choice from the other ones listed.

Keisha got in her silver Chrysler 300 C and shut the door blocking out the cool December wind. Before she started her car, she glanced down at the picture of her family she was still holding in her hand. David, the kids, and her looked so happy. So content. They appeared to be the picture of a perfect family but, within their perfection, there were flaws. They were imperfections only Keisha was aware of and, as far as she was concerned, she wanted to keep it that way. She didn't care to bother David with the various issues and problems she'd been dealing with. She would rather keep everything stable, the way it had been. Having such stability and peace among her family unit was extremely important and the very thing she strived hard to maintain even if it meant scheduling appointments around her job and having all her medical bills sent directly to her desk at work. She deemed it necessary.

Keisha knew she wasn't right for withholding such serious information from her spouse but didn't feel comfortable telling him. Didn't feel comfortable telling anyone. She could barely even open up to Karen who she was paying, out of her pocket, to help her work through her problems. Granted, she had only been to her therapist a couple of times but she still wasn't ready to be completely open with her yet.

On the drive home, Keisha began to think about what her therapist said. She knew she was more than wrong for not answering Aunt Darlene's phone calls but something within her wouldn't let her. It was almost as if she had a mental block preventing her from talking to her aunt all together.

Keisha also thought about how crazy she must've looked when she told Karen she had no desire to keep in touch with Darlene and Jessie. She was serious about wanting nothing to do with them. When she left Columbus, nine years ago, she decided to leave all of her memories and all of the people involved behind. She never knew her grandmother because Rita told her she died before Keisha could even remember her. As for surviving family, Darlene and Jessie was all she had so when she left the area she initially found it quite easy to separate herself from them.

For close to six years, Keisha had been successful at keeping her distance but, one day shortly after she had just married, she received a phone call out of the blue from her aunt. Keisha recognized the Columbus area code and knew it had to be Darlene.

"How did you get my new number?" Keisha asked as soon as she picked up the phone.

"Is that how you greet me after all these years?"

"Aunt Darlene, how did you get this number? It's private and unlisted." Keisha sighed and held the phone away from her ear for a moment while she stared at the familiar number and caught an attitude all over again. She could still hear her aunt on the other end so she knew she wasn't imagining things yet Darlene was so persistent she wouldn't hang up until she said everything she had to say anyway.

Keisha knew she was being cold toward her aunt but she had worked hard, back and forth with the telephone company, to make sure her number wasn't accessible to the public so she was confused as to how her aunt was able to get it so easily. If the phone company made that mistake, Keisha was definitely going to contact them to get her money back.

"Your sister Kennedi gave it to me."

"What do you want?" Keisha asked as she rolled her eyes. She made a personal mental note to deal with her sister later.

"I heard you just got married and I wanted to call and say congratulations."

"Yeah, I just got married. Thanks," she replied. The emotion drained completely from her voice. She desperately hoped her aunt would get the point but she continued to carry on conversation like they were old friends.

"Well, I must say your uncle and I are proud."

"Is that all you called to say?"

"Yeah, well, I wanted to know…" Keisha pressed the end button on the phone and slammed it down on the table before

Darlene could open up her mouth and tell her anything else. She preferred to keep her conversations with Darlene very short and straight to the point. If Keisha had her way, she would never speak to Darlene or Jessie again.

Keisha pulled her car into the driveway, as her mind drifted back into present time, and realized her husband had already made it home. She was surprised because usually she arrived first but ended up having a longer session than normal. She parked her car in its usual spot in the garage, walked up the three wooden steps, and opened the door directly connected to the kitchen. From the moment she walked into the kitchen, the smell of spaghetti entered into her nostrils. She was relieved David took the initiative to cook dinner. Keisha felt she was too mentally exhausted to whip up a meal, not to mention the fact that David was an incredible cook and could basically put together anything. Most of the time, Keisha stepped to the side and let him flex his culinary muscles.

She walked into the kitchen with a huge smile on her face, felt so blessed to have a man like him. He was always doing things to make her life easier. It made her feel like she was the most special woman in the world. Sometimes she wondered what she had done to deserve a man like him. He seemed to make everything wrong in her life right, the exact opposite of every man she encountered and that is what drew her to him when they were in college. She met David at an ice breaker party when she was a freshman and he was a sophomore. Since she was new on campus, she made it a point to attend every social function she could to meet more people and ended up finding him in the process. The chemistry between them was so natural and, from the first moment, the attraction was instant. They've practically been joined at the hip ever since.

"Baby, it's smellin' good in here. Is that what I think it is?" Keisha walked up to David and wrapped her arms around his muscular frame while he stood over the stove stirring the pot of noodles.

"It sure is. Been a long time since we had some spaghetti and I wanted to cook something quick for us all to eat because we have church tonight."

"Oh," Keisha replied as she rolled her eyes behind his back so he couldn't pickup on the instant attitude she developed.

"Yeah. We have bible study tonight and I want us to be on time so we don't miss anything. You wanna come with me and the kids tonight?" Dave asked but Keisha scrunched her lips and nose together as she appeared to have smelled a foul odor. David raised his eyebrows with a perplexed expression.

"No babe, you know church just isn't my thing. Why don't you and the kids go and enjoy yourself? Oooh…this pasta looks so good I wanna taste it," Keisha said, trying to quickly change the subject.

David knew she changed the subject on purpose because, when he brought up anything about going to church or the Lord, she always found a way to conveniently switch topics and was quite successful at it. His strong belief in the Lord was also the very reason why they almost broke off their engagement because Keisha really didn't agree with him attending church so much. It wasn't that she opposed him going to church all together but, when he attended, he always went on a personal crusade to get her to come with him while Keisha wasn't feeling it at all. She actually became so irritated that she almost told him where to go and what do with his religion. But, after thinking everything over and coming to her senses, she concluded not to pass up a good man like David over something as simple as him being a Christian. So her way of dealing with it turned into her trying to avoid the subject as much as she could.

"You sure you don't wanna go with me and the kids? It would be nice to go as a family."

"Naw, I'm good. Now I really want to have a taste of what the love of my life cooked for dinner?" Keisha said.

David decided not to press the issue. Instead, he stuck a fork in the pot of spaghetti and twirled it around in a circular motion until he had enough noodles to give her a little taste.

He held his hand underneath the steaming fork and blew on it to cool the pasta down. After it was ready, David lifted the fork to Keisha's mouth. He smiled as she closed her eyes and enjoyed every bite.

"David, you put your foot in this spaghetti."

"You like it, baby?" he asked as he laughed slightly at her facial expressions.

"You already know what I'm gonna say. It tastes wonderful. I'm ready to eat. Where are the twins?" Keisha asked as she looked around and didn't see her children.

"I just sent them upstairs to wash up for dinner. They smell like crayons and glue," David replied and they both laughed.

"Now you know why I make them take a bath as soon as they hit the door."

"That's exactly why," David replied and then snapped his finger and then pointed at her, indicating he'd just remembered something.

"Babe, before I forget. Aunt Darlene called for you. She said it's real important. She wants you to call her back," David said. Keisha rolled her eyes.

"Whatever, I'm not calling that lady back."

"Baby, why you act like that every time she calls you? That is your aunt and it's not like the two of you talk all the time."

"I don't care who Darlene thinks she is. She's not my aunt and I'm not calling her back!" Keisha stated as her mood shifted from calmness to utter irritation. Not knowing what else to say, he held up his hands to surrender.

"Sorry, didn't mean to make you upset. I know how angry you get when I bring up Darlene's name up so I apologize. I just wanted to tell you she called."
Keisha took a deep breath, paused, and then changed her tone.

"Look David, I'm sorry for snappin' on you for no reason. I just don't have a desire to talk to that woman. At all!"

"It's okay. Sure you don't wanna go to service tonight with me and the kids?"

"No, I'll pass. Let's eat before the food gets cold."

Keisha sat down at the table with David and the kids to enjoy the delicious meal he prepared. Their previous discussion about the unwanted phone call ceased and they began to talk to Katrina and D.J. about their day at school. But, the entire time at dinner Keisha couldn't stop thinking about Darlene calling for her. The last time she called, after she got married to David, Keisha made up in her mind that she would never speak to Darlene or Jessie again. Keisha's thoughts wondered while her children talked to the point where she was unable to concentrate on what they said. She couldn't seem to figure out why Darlene's attempting to contact her after all these years and what it is she actually wanted but knew one thing was for sure. She didn't care either way.

# chapter 2

Keisha decided to tidy up the house once David and the kids left. She figured this would be the perfect time to straighten up while her dynamic duo was gone, because it was usually so hard to clean when they were home because she usually found herself continuously going up behind them so nothing was ever completed.

She began picking up magazines that cluttered up her coffee table and ran across the piece of paper with "Darlene" scribbled at the top in her husband's chicken scratch. The name was practically illegible but she could read the numbers clearly. Keisha shook her head back and forth as she stared at it.

I don't even know why she gave me her number when I already know it by heart. It hasn't changed since we first moved with them. She act like I forgot or somethin. I haven't forgotten. I just don't call.

Keisha looked at the number and thought about what her therapist told her just earlier that day.

The next time Darlene calls you I want you to pick it up. I think it would be good for you to talk to her.

She remembered promising Dr. Karen to at least try and pick up the phone if Darlene called again but, the way she felt, she wasn't sure if she wanted to talk to her. Honestly, the piece of advice sounded like it was read verbatim out of one of those counseling handbooks and Keisha couldn't say she agreed with it one bit.

A knock at her front door interrupted her silent conversation and, by the way the person banged on the door, she knew it could only be one person - her baby sister Kennedi. She was the only one who insisted on knocking like they still lived in the hood where it was always noisy. She had told her time and time again to get some good sense but Kennedi never seemed to remember. When Keisha opened up her door, she saw her sister standing there with a head full of platinum blonde weave. The sight alone caused her to giggle. She tried not to burst out in laughter but her chocolate brown sister wearing the brightest hair she could find in the hair store was entirely too funny for her to try holding on the inside.

"Keesh, what took you so long to answer? That's unlike you."

"What in the world is that up in your head?" Keisha asked as Kennedi walked in the house and closed the door behind her.

"It's my new hairstyle. You like?" Kennedi asked as she stroked a few strands of synthetic hair with her hand. Keisha couldn't even respond to her sister until she stopped laughing.

"Kennedi, first off, the hair is platinum blonde which is not even close to your real hair color then you're wearing it super long."

"You don't like it? I wanted to try something new. I think it makes me look like Lil Kim... I know you seen me on the video," Kennedi smiled while Keisha couldn't stop laughing at her sister's foolish antics. The sad thing is she knew her baby sister was being serious and really thought she resembled the platinum selling rapper.

"Well try, try again!" Keisha continued to laugh.
Kennedi smacked her super glossed up lips outlined with black liner, which was another thing Keisha had an issue with. She don't know how many times she told Kennedi that, although wearing the black and brown lip liner on your lips with plain lip gloss was in style in the nineties, this was definitely not in style now and those days were long gone. No matter how much Keisha said this to Kennedi, she still insisted on tracing her lips with black liner and threw on a coat of lip gloss over it like she was being a trendsetter on something. Most of the time, Keisha just tossed her hands up in surrender to her sister who would do her own thing anyway regardless of what anyone said.

"Oh quit bein' a hater. You wish you could wear your hair like dis!" Kennedi replied and followed Keisha into living room where they sat next to each other on the couch.

"Believe me sis I'm not hating on you. Not hating at all. Where's my little man Quincy?"

Before Kennedi answered her sister, she rolled her eyes which let Keisha know she was about to be in for a story.

"Quincy is wit his dad at home. I left him there. I needed some me time."

"What did Lil Quincy do now?" Keisha inquired.

"It's not what he did. It's what his daddy isn't doin'."

"What's Big Quincy doing now?" Keisha couldn't say she was surprised at all because he always did something to make Kennedi mad. Keisha was still shocked that they were together.

"He's doin' nothing."

"What?"

"You heard me. He's not doing anything. Not for me... not for Quincy. He would rather sit in front of that Xbox 360 all day than work a nine to five and I'm tired of it!" Kennedi crossed her arms.

"Tired of what?"

"Tired of him not taking care of us the way he should. I'm tired of bustin' my behind at some dead end job while he's at home doin' nothing."

"So is Quincy trying to find work?" Keisha asked as her sister began to snicker.

"Humph! He gon' have to after what I just did," Kennedi replied as she looked away.

Keisha tried to study her sister's body language to see what it revealed but couldn't quite read her. Either way she didn't have a good feeling.

"Oh my goodness! What did you do?" Keisha asked.

"Well, let's just say, he's forced to start looking for a job."

"Please don't tell me."

"Yup, I quit mine!" Kennedi smiled as if she accomplished a major feat.

"Why would you do that?" Keisha asked. She was eager to hear what her sister had to say. She already knew there was a high probability her answer wouldn't make the least bit of sense but she allowed her to continue on.

"I quit because I'm sick of that job. I can't stand the people and, if I continue to work, Quincy won't be motivated to find a job. So, I did what I felt I had to do."

"But why would you quit when technically you're the only income in your household. And, on top of that, you don't even have anything else lined up?" Keisha took a deep breath and exhaled, which indicated she was mad. She couldn't believe her sister would make a move like that without weighing the consequences first. But then again, her sister always seemed to be doing something with absolutely no meaning behind it.

"I know my move was a bit drastic but I'm fed up with our situation. Besides, it's like they say... drastic times, call for drastic measures."

"So now you're into philosophy?"

"No, but I'm just saying he better step up or me and Lil Quincy are out!" Kennedi smacked her lips. Keisha attempted to open her mouth and reply to her sister's last comment but decided to leave it alone.

She didn't know why Kennedi tried to act all big, bad, and bold, tossing out ultimatums when Quincy had been unemployed since the day they met each other five years ago. As long as they'd been together, the man never worked longer than two weeks. And, when you asked him what he planned on doing with his life, all he talked about was sending out his demo tape and landing a record deal. Nothing changed with Quincy so she honestly couldn't understand why her sister would think it would be any different now.

"Okay Kennedi, but I just hope you know what you're doing. You know I worry about you and my nephew."

"I know sis but we'll be fine," Kennedi reassured her.

"On to other news, you know Darlene been calling here the past few days trying to get a hold of me."

"Well, did you talk to her to see what she wants?" Kennedi asked.

"Why should I? I don't have any desire to talk to that woman."

"Aunt Darlene said she's been trying to call you but you haven't returned any of her phone calls. It's really important."

"What is so important that she feels the need to call me when she knows good and well I don't want to speak to her?"

"Uncle Jessie is sick. That's why she's been trying to call you," she blurted out.

"So! I don't care. Why did she want to call and tell me that? What he got the flu, a cold or something?" Keisha asked while studying her sister's serious facial expression.

"No Keisha. He's dying."

"Dying? What are you talking about?"

Kennedi took a long pause while she stared at the ground searching for the right words to say. When she finally composed her thoughts, she continued to speak.

"It's his organs. Well, actually his diabetes is getting worse and his organs are failing. His kidneys are shutting down so his prognosis isn't good at all," Kennedi explained.

Keisha sat there and processed everything she'd just been told. Her mind began to race as she thought about what Kennedi said.

"Well, I hope Darlene wasn't calling me because she wanted me to have some type of sympathy on that man because I don't. As far as I'm concerned, good riddens!"

She knew she came off callous toward her family but she didn't care. Even though there was a part of her wanting to show some form of compassion, another side of her wouldn't let her be that transparent.

"Keisha, please don't be that way. Darlene and Jessie are still our aunt and uncle. You can't say something like that when the man is really sick."

"Why can't I? They aren't any aunt and uncle of mine. It's been that way since I first moved in with them back in the day."

"I know but I really hope you consider talking to Darlene because what's going on is serious."

Keisha understood Kennedi's point of view about Darlene and Jessie but she was also aware of the fact her comments were one-sided. She knew, to her sister, she must sound like a cold-blooded and heartless person because her sister didn't know the real reason behind her feelings. Nobody knew the truth hiding behind her tough exterior.

Shortly after her sister left, David and the kids returned from church. The kids told her about what they had learned in the Bible study. David began to load up his truck with the UPS shipment of items he received for his barber shop and Keisha decided to catch up on some episodes of Young and the

Restless she'd taped on TV when their house phone began to ring.

She picked up the phone to glance at the caller ID but, when she saw Darlene's number pop up on the screen, she developed an instant attitude. She let the phone ring several times before she pressed the "talk" button on the cordless phone although she really wasn't overly anxious to talk to her since receiving the heads up from Kennedi.

"Hello? Is Keisha there?" Darlene asked. Instead of answering her, Keisha took the phone away from her ear and hung it up. She didn't feel like talking to her at that moment and was glad she didn't open up her mouth to say anything. She continued on with watching her soap opera then David came in to join her.

"Hey baby, who was that calling? I heard the phone ringing while I was putting those boxes in the trunk."

"Oh it wasn't anybody. They had the wrong number."

She knew she shouldn't lie to her husband about something so superficial but she didn't want to explain herself and definitely wasn't in the mood for another spiritual lecture.

# chapter 3

Keisha tossed and turned the majority of the night while David slept peacefully next to her. Memories of the past clouded her thoughts like fog and caused a storm of emotions to come over her. It seemed like the more she tried to relax the more things occurred in her mind. At first, she was able to fall asleep when David came upstairs and got in bed with her but, after two hours, her eyes popped open as if they were on their own personal schedule. The constant stirring in her bed caused her to become frustrated and she stopped trying to fight with herself.

If she wasn't battling with herself, she tussled with the covers - their Egyptian cotton sheets and comforter that felt like chains and weights being wrapped around her body. She usually found complete solace in their king size bed and often had to be peeled away when it was time to wake up and this wasn't the case. It was like everything in the room bothered her. The alarm clock's big, red numbers seemed to keep her eyes open and illuminate the room with its bold and rich color. She took it and turned it against the wall, hoping that would solve her problem but, when it didn't because she swore she could hear the time change with each passing minute, she unplugged the device and let it drop to the floor.

Her husband's breathing and light snoring was another source of irritation for her. Normally, she wouldn't have heard him at all but, since she found herself up at such a late hour, his usual undetectable noises sounded like a grizzly bear laid next to her. She nudged him several times to get him to move until she couldn't hear him anymore but that didn't work either.

Keisha honestly wished Darlene and Jessie would just leave her alone so she could have a normal life but they obviously weren't that courteous. By the time the sun came up, she barely slept two hours. She didn't spring out of bed like she normally did when she woke up yet drug herself out of it, freshened up and went downstairs to cook a quick breakfast for everyone.

"Good morning mommy," the twins said in unison as they entered the kitchen together.

"Good morning babies. I made you some breakfast." Keisha fixed them both a plate of eggs, bacon, and toast. She let out a loud yawn as she fixed both their plates.

"Mommy are you okay? You look sick," Katrina said as Keisha placed her food in front of her.

"No, I'm okay. I just need to get some rest," Keisha replied and dropped a sandwich into each of their lunch boxes before David came down the steps and wrapped his arms around Keisha. He kissed her on the cheek.

"Baby, I know you're off today so I'll take the kids to school on my way to the shop," he said as she handed him his plate of food.

"Thanks babe. I'll pick them up since you're taking them. I appreciate that honey." Keisha let out another yawn.

"Did you get some rest last night? You look sleepy," David said as he put his food down and stroked the side of his wife's face.

"No, not really, but I'll be okay. I plan on getting some in a little while." Keisha poured David a glass of cranberry juice. She knew she was exhausted but, if one more person told her she looked tired, she was going to be mad.

"Yeah, you need to get some rest so you can enjoy what I have planned later." David released a sneaky smile, which let Keisha know her husband had something up his sleeve. Keisha leaned and kissed him softly on the lips.

"In that case, I'm going to get extra rest."

"You do that."

Keisha attempted to relax on her day off but, every time she planned to sit down and relax, she ended up finding something else to do. If it wasn't that, then the house phone rang.

She decided to unplug her unruly phone until it behaved then found her a comfortable spot on the couch only to hear someone knocking. As she walked to her front door, she hoped it wasn't her sister Kennedi. Although she loved her dearly, she realized she could only tolerate Kennedi in small spurts.

"Hey Alonzo, what brings you over my way?" Keisha asked as she saw her eldest brother standing on her stoop with his back turned to her. He turned around and smiled.

"Hey you! What up sis?" Alonzo said as he reached out and hugged her. Keisha embraced him and smelled cigarette smoke on his clothes. She also noticed that he hadn't gotten his hair cut in a while because his nice grade appeared to have a nappy texture. This type of appearance was unlike her brother who prided himself in being clean cut.

"Come in bro. It's cold out there." She stepped to the side and let Alonzo pass her to walk into the house. Keisha closed the front door and locked it while he stood in the foyer, rubbing his hands together, trying to restore some warmth to them.

"Thanks sis. I'm glad I caught you at home. I've been meaning to come see you."

"Yeah. It's been a little while," Keisha replied as she started to walk into the living room but stopped dead in her tracks when she saw Alonzo still had on his Timberland boots.

"Oh yeah, I forgot you're Miss Particular!" Alonzo stepped out of his shoes and placed them next to the stairs.

"Shut up, Alonzo," Keisha warned as he held up his hands letting her know she's won the fight.

"So what brings you all the way over here to see me?" Keisha asked.

"What you mean sis? I came over here because I wanted to catch up with you."

"For real? So you're telling me you came over here to just see how I was doing?"

"Yeah Keesh, it's been a while since I've seen you, David and the kids. Speaking of, where are my niece and nephew at?"

Keisha wondered the true reason for Alonzo's surprise visit. Her brother wasn't the type to frequently visit so she knew one of two things was going on: either he was in trouble or he needed something. At this point, she wasn't able to put her finger on exactly which one it was but she had never been wrong.

"The twins are at school and you know where David is."

"That's cool. Business good for him?"

"Yeah extremely good. They've almost tripled their clientele since they added onto the shop. He and his partner just brought the property next door so they can expand it even further."

"That's what's up. I ain't mad at all," he said.

Keisha heard his stomach growl.

"You hungry? Want me to fix you something?"

Alonzo shook his head.

"Naw, I'm good."

"Come on Zo. I just heard your stomach. Besides, I'm off work today so I can cook you something. It's no problem."

"You don't have to cook sis. I'm alright."

"Quit turnin' me down. I wanna cook something for you," Keisha replied as she walked into the kitchen. Alonzo followed suite right behind her.

"Well, since you put it like that, I'll eat if you cook me something. You don't have to beg," he answered with a slight laugh then took a seat at the island.

While Keisha prepared some lunch, they caught up on everything that had gone on since the last time they saw each other. For some reason, a sense of nervousness resonated from Alonzo as she spoke. The uneasiness seemed to escape through his words during their conversation and Keisha couldn't ignore it any longer.

"Zo, is everything cool with you? You seem tense." Keisha observed Alonzo tapping his right leg feverishly on the floor.

He snickered again at his sister's words.

"I told you sis. Everything is cool. I'm not nervous. Nervous about what? I'm fine," Alonzo replied, satisfied with his answer, but Keisha detected the total opposite. She knew something was wrong with him. She could feel it.

"Okay, now, don't lie to me 'cuz you know I always have a way of finding out anyway." Keisha stared at her brother.

"Yeah, nothing gets past you Agent Private Eye!" Alonzo laughed and tapped on both of his pant pockets like he was searching for something.

"Sis, I'll be right back. I think I left my phone in the car." Alonzo got up and started to walk out when something dropped out of his pocket. Keisha walked over to the box of cigarettes and picked them up before Alonzo could even bend down.

"You start smoking again?" Keisha asked as she held the green and white box in her hand.

"Since last month."

"You only smoke when you're stressed. You sure you're telling me the truth?"

Alonzo reached for the box and placed it back inside of this pocket.

"I promise, I'm fine Keesh. It's just a little bad habit that I pick up from time to time. That's all," Alonzo tried to reassure.

Keisha shook her head at her brother then stared at him one good time before she responded. "Okay bro, whatever you say."

She didn't care if he tried to reassure her or not, her intuition told her there was more to the story than he let on. She didn't know what was really going on but she figured it wouldn't be long before she found out. After

Alonzo finished eating, he decided to ride with Keisha to pick up the kids from school.

When Katrina and D.J. saw their uncle sitting in the passenger's seat of their mom's car, they practically broke their necks trying to get to him.

"Uncle Alonzo! Uncle Alonzo! We missed you!" They screamed back and forth as if they were competing with each other.

"Hey, my favorite niece and nephew. What's up?" he replied as the kids took their places in the backseat and shut the door. The ride back home was noisy. The twins talked to their uncle the entire way home and, by the time Keisha pulled into the driveway, she was glad they'd made it home. Before they could say anything else, Keisha shut them down.

"Babies, can you please go in the house and leave your uncle alone? Go upstairs and start your homework, I'll be up in a little bit." Keisha looked in the mirror at her children who seemed to be crushed by what she'd just told them.

"Okay mommy," Katrina answered with her head down.

"Bye Uncle Lonzo!" D.J. replied as they both disappeared into the house.    "Excuse your niece and nephew. They get little carried away sometimes."

"It's cool. I love Katrina and D.J. I like hearing what they have to say."

"I do too but they get on my last good nerve sometimes. I love them dearly but they can also take me over the edge too!" Keisha put the car in park and slid the key out of the ignition but Alonzo grabbed her arm before she could move.

"Okay, remember I told you everything was cool and I didn't need anything? Well, I do need something," Alonzo said with a serious look on his face.

"What do you need?" Keisha said as he validated her initial intuition.

Alonzo took a deep breath and released the air occupying his lungs. Keisha knew she was in for an interesting request.

"Look Keesh, before you shut me down just hear me out okay?" he explained. She nodded her head for him to continue.

"I'm listening," Keisha replied as she crossed her arms over her chest.

"Alright, I've never been one to beat around the bush so I'm just gon' say it. I need some money, Keisha, and I was wondering if you and Dave can give me a loan."

"Depends on how much it is."

"Three thousand," Alonzo confessed and then looked away.

"Oh, you're crazy! You mean to tell me you need Dave and I to loan you three thousand dollars? We don't have that type of money to toss around. What you need it for?" Keisha asked with a suspicious look on her face.

Alonzo held up his hand.

"I can't really tell you why but I need it"

"Alonzo, are you gambling again?" Keisha stared at him without turning away. She could see the look of shock on his face as if she just said something she wasn't supposed to but that was the only thing she could come up with to ask him.

He shook his head back and forth in disagreement of her accusation.

"Naw sis, I'm not gambling. I stopped that a long time ago. Why would you say that?" Alonzo raised his eyebrows surprised at his sister's accusation.

"I dunno. That's the only thing I can think of as to why you need three thousand dollars."

Keisha's mind traveled back to two years ago when Alonzo was addicted to gambling. He even had his own business and was making good money as an insurance agent to support his girlfriend and child until his habit got the best of him. Before he knew it, he'd loss everything he owned from his business to all of the money he'd saved when he was in the Navy. He ended up losing his family as well.

Up until then, he claimed to never have a problem with gambling but, when he lost everything, it was the wake-up call he needed to put himself in rehab and get his life together. Once released, he swore up and down to be a changed man but there was always some incident that would alert Keisha to the fact Alonzo still dabbled in the gambling.

"I know you automatically thinking that but, I'm telling you, it's not that at all."

"Then, why can't you tell me the real reason why you need this money?"

"Because I can't. Just trust me on this. I just need the loan and I promise I'll get it back to you," Alonzo pleaded while Keisha looked him up and down like he was crazy.

"If you won't even tell me why you need this money, then I'm sorry there's nothing I can do. So are you gonna tell me what you need it for or not?"

"Keisha, I can't."

"Well, I'm sorry bro but I won't be able to help you out this time. You know I would if I could," Keisha explained as she held her hands up not knowing what else to tell him. Alonzo inhaled and took a deep breath as he digested his sister's final answer.

"Alright sis I understand. Well, look, I gotta run. Kiss the twins for me and I'll see you around." He placed a kiss on her forehead then got out of her car.

As she watched her brother pull out of the driveway in his white Buick Park Avenue, she felt bad. Keisha wished she could help him out with his money problem but, without a real reason, she couldn't do anything. She usually never hesitated to help her brother in the past but lending a helping hand to him over the years had caused too many fights and arguments between her and her husband and Keisha grew tired of explaining to David where money was going. She knew this time wouldn't be any different and she desired to keep the peace at all cost so her brother would to have to find a way to get three thousand dollars on his own.

# chapter 4

"Hello," Keisha said as she opened her cell phone and placed it between her ear and shoulder. Normally she wouldn't answer her phone while at work and but was on her lunch break, sitting at her desk.

"Keisha, is that you?" Darlene asked.

Here it was. The moment Keisha dreaded the most, Darlene's phone call. She'd been avoiding her for about a week and a half since she called the house and had no intentions of calling back.

"Hey Darlene," she responded dryly.

"I'm so glad I have you on the phone. You're such a hard person to get in touch with."

"Yeah, I know. What's up?" Keisha rolled her eyes. She wished her aunt could see her gestures through the phone then maybe she would hang up and never think to contact again. She stared down at the chicken salad she'd ordered for lunch and pushed it away from her. She was extremely hungry but, after hearing her aunt's voice, she slowly lost her appetite.

"I bet you're real excited to talk to me huh?" Darlene asked in a sarcastic tone. Keisha sucked her teeth and switched her phone to the other side.

"Extremely ecstatic. I mean... you're the one who called so obviously you want to talk to me." Keisha hoped she would get straight to the point because she didn't believe in beating around the bush at all.

"I do want to speak with you but I would rather see you face to face."

"Why? I'm on the phone right now. You can tell me whatever it is you have to say," Keisha stated as she finally decided to put the lid container back on her salad.

"I know I can, Keisha, but there are some serious things I want to tell you in person."

"Well, I'm sorry but I don't think I'm coming to Columbus any time soon and, besides, I haven't been there for nine years. I don't believe that's gonna happen."

"It's about your uncle. He's very sick and I would like for you to come and visit us," Darlene explained.

"No! I don't think that's possible." Keisha didn't know how many times she was going to say no to Darlene before she got the hint but was prepared to continue saying it until she comprehended.

"Keisha look... I know we haven't always had the best relationship in the world but I'm asking you. No, I'm begging you to please come home and visit. Your uncle had to have surgery and the only person he's been asking for since his anesthesia wore off was you."

Why am I not surprised? It seems like he lives and breathes to make my life difficult.

"Okay, but the way I feel right now I don't care if the president asked for me. It still doesn't mean I have to come running."

Keisha was fully aware that her statement was colder than ice but she didn't care at all. She could hear her aunt on the other end of the phone sniffing, which probably meant she was crying, and that was the last thing Keisha wanted to hear.

"Keisha, I really need to see you," Darlene said and then paused. Keisha sighed and then began to look up in the air. She did see a couple of her co-workers come from their offices to see what all the commotion was about but signaled that she was fine so they returned to what they were doing.

"Look, if I come home, will you leave me alone?" Keisha asked.

"Yes, I just really need to see you."

"Alright, well I'm on my way."

Keisha ended the call, jumped on the internet to book a hotel room, and mentally prepared herself to go to the very place she didn't want to go.

Later that afternoon, after Keisha got off work, she came home and got her things ready for the trip to Columbus. Her sister's boyfriend ended up taking the kids to the movies after they got out of school and agreed to keep them over the weekend since Lil Quincy wanted them to spend the night over their house. That arrangement worked out fine due to the fact that David's clientele tended to be pretty heavy on the weekends since his shop decided to accept walk-ins. On Saturdays, they usually kept a line wrapping around the walls waiting customers who wanted to get their hair cut.

"Baby, are you sure you don't want me to take you? I can always reschedule my Saturday appointments," Dave said as he loaded Keisha's overnight bag into the trunk and slammed it shut.

"No it's fine. You don't have to change your schedule for me. I'm just going down for the weekend and I'm coming straight back. I'm not staying long at all," Keisha reassured.

"I know babe, but you know that I'll cancel to be with you," Dave replied and smiled at his beautiful wife. Keisha leaned in and kissed him. She was so glad her husband was supportive of everything she did and would drop his plans just to be with her. Even though she would rather have him by her side when she went to Columbus, she needed to take this trip by herself. Although her husband knew of her family, he had never met them and Keisha worked hard to keep it that way. She didn't want David to meet the two people she couldn't stand the most and preferred to not even talk about them at all when they spoke of their families. He would ask her from time to time about Darlene and Jessie but she constantly changed the subject. She usually didn't care what she had to do but she tried to avert that topic at all cost.

"I know you would take the day off to be with me and that's why I love you. But, I'm cool baby. I'll drive myself and be back before you know it." Keisha kissed him again.

"I love you too and I'm glad you're finally going home to visit. I know they'll be happy to see you," David replied. He pulled her in close to him and kissed her one more time before she said goodbye and got in her car.

David stood in the driveway and waved as she drove off. She knew he and her sister were glad she finally decided to visit Darlene and Jessie but she wasn't happy about it at all. Going to the place where she lived as a child didn't excite her in the least bit and she was content on never returning. Traveling there produced uneasiness in her stomach because deep down inside she always tried to forget it existed.

Keisha didn't know how much of a good idea it was to be going home but it was too late to consider her actions because, by the time she realized she had been daydreaming, she pulled into the subdivision of the upscale suburban neighborhood where they lived. The two hour drive from Akron to Columbus seemed to only have lasted minutes and she had arrived much quicker than expected.

The closer she got to the house the faster her heart beat. She even recognized her breathing becoming more erratic.

"Okay Keisha. Calm down. Quit trippin. Just be cool. Everything will be fine," she said out loud to herself in between taking deep breaths. The way her natural body reacted to entering the neighborhood was the same way she felt when Darlene and Jessie had first brought them to their house after they took custody.

Keisha remembered how her eyes lit up as they turned into the area which had hundreds of brand new homes with manicured lawns. She became mesmerized when she saw so many pretty houses. She never remembered any houses looking like that where she was from. She had only previously seen a neighborhood like it on television.

"Where are we going?" Keisha asked as she continued to stare out the window at the beautiful sight.

"We're taking you to our home," Darlene replied and smiled.

"Y'all live here?" Alonzo asked.

"Yes we do. We live right here," Jessie said as he pulled their van into the driveway of a two-story home with grass resembling a golf course. Keisha hopped out the van and stood in the middle of the driveway taking in everything. She couldn't believe they were about to live in a house that pretty. She didn't have any friends even close to living in a house this nice. It was completely different from the raggedy apartment complex they had called home for so many years. Keisha felt dreamy walking into the house and didn't ever want to wake up. It was as if they were living in a fairytale and she hoped it would continue but soon, after they moved in, things definitely changed.

Keisha's cell phone began to ring as she pulled into the driveway, snapping her out of her thoughts.

"Hey babe, I was just calling to see where you were," David said as Keisha balanced the phone on her shoulder. She tried to pull completely into the driveway but it snowed so much the night before she kept getting stuck. And instead of trying to drive up further, Keisha put her car in park and decided to leave it there.

"What's going on over there? I hear a lot of noise," David asked.

"It snowed last night. There is so much snow in this driveway, I almost got stuck."

"It wasn't supposed to snow for almost a week down there."

"Yeah I know but I'm about to go up in here and see what's going on."

"You cool honey? I told you I would've cancelled my appointments to be with you. I can still come if you need me."

"Don't bother David. As soon as I'm done with Darlene, I'm going to the hotel and I'll be home tomorrow."

"Okay, well, call me later. Love you."

"I love you more." Keisha pressed the red button on her phone to end the call and placed it back in her holster clip.

Before she got out of the car, she stared at the house she lived in for so many years and couldn't believe it snowed so much. Granted, it always snowed in Columbus, but she never remembered it snowing as much in the past and couldn't understand why it was snowing this much at that moment. She also couldn't understand why she was at Darlene's when she promised herself she would never return to this place again.

Keisha took a deep breath, got out of her car, and made the short walk up to the front door where she pressed the doorbell. Darlene must've been anticipating her arrival because the bell hadn't finished ringing and she was already opening the door.

"Oh my Lord, Keisha, it's you! I'm so happy to see you. It's been a long time." Darlene said as tears began to well up in her eyes. Darlene opened the screen door and held out her arms to give Keisha a hug but she stiffened her entire body to cancel the advance. Darlene's super excited mood was knocked down several levels so she closed the door and locked it. Keisha briefly looked at Darlene but didn't say anything. She didn't know what to say to end the awkwardness between them but knew it wouldn't be long before her aunt said something else.

"I'm just glad you're home," Darlene said. Keisha replied with a half smile which consisted of pressing her lips together quickly. "I thought you might be a little hungry from being on the road so I made you something to eat," Darlene continued, hoping that alone would be enough to spark somewhat of a conversation between them.

"Okay," Keisha said as she followed Darlene through the hallway to the kitchen. As she walked through the house, her mind began to go back to the time when she, Alonzo, and Kennedi lived with them. Even though it had been a while since she had been there, Keisha noticed the décor hadn't changed much while her mind became flooded with so many memories she didn't even hear Darlene asking her what she wanted.

"Keisha, did you hear me? I asked did you want some of these chicken and dumplings?"

"I don't care," she replied unenthusiastically.

"Well, I'll take that as a yes." She poured some of the food she made into a glass bowl and put it in the microwave.

While it was heating up, Darlene started to talk again. She walked over to where Keisha sat at the kitchen table and took a seat across from her. She placed her hands in front of her and clasped them together.

"You're uncle is very sick, Keisha. He's been in the hospital on and off for the past year and a half."

"What's wrong with Jessie now?" Keisha asked as Darlene handed her the food. She was glad her food was ready to eat because she figured she could make herself be preoccupied with eating rather than acting like she was concerned with Jessie's well being. She really didn't care to know what he was going through at the particular moment. She didn't care at all.

"You know he's been diabetic for a long time but now it's starting to affect his organs. He started going into kidney failure last year and his condition has been deteriorating ever since."

# pretty skeletons

Darlene paused, trying to get herself together, but tears had already escaped and began to run down her chestnut colored cheeks. Keisha didn't even bother to look up at her aunt when she talked. She continued on with eating savoring every bite as if she ate a world class, four-star meal. She knew it was wrong to not stop to empathize with Darlene but, at that point, she didn't know what else to say.

"So why haven't his doctor put him on dialysis yet?"

"That's the problem. They have and dialysis worked for a while but over the last three months it hasn't been successful at all." Darlene reached in the middle of the table and grabbed a tissue. Keisha started to get annoyed at the fact her aunt was being a complete water head. Although she cried, Keisha still didn't look up at her. She wasn't in the mood to console Darlene. She didn't even want to be there, truthfully as she made the choice to visit only because of all the flack she'd been catching lately. She actually could tolerate her aunt. It was Jessie who she couldn't stand.

Darlene's cell phone began to buzz on the countertop and she flipped it open and said, "Hello."

From the way her face began to shine with illumination, Keisha figured she was talking to her loser of a husband. Her skin began to crawl at the thought of him being on the other end.

"Yeah, Jessie, she just got here," she answered. On that note, Keisha got up from the table and walked out of the kitchen. She wanted to finish the rest of her food but just knowing her aunt was on the other line with that idiot made her somewhat nauseous. She walked down the short hallway with shiny wooden floors and went into the bathroom until she heard Darlene wrapping up her phone call. Then, she returned. "Why did you walk away, your uncle wanted to speak to you?"

"Now, you know, I don't have anything to say to that man."

"But, he wanted to speak to you Keisha."

"Darlene, I don't care," Keisha replied and took the plate of food and headed toward the trash can.

"You're about the throw your food away. I thought you were hungry?"

Keisha continued to the trash can where she began scraping her plate. "I suddenly lost my appetite."

Darlene shook her head and then glanced down at her Coach watch.

"Well, I'm thinking we can get over to the hospital and sit with Jessie until visiting hours are over," she suggested to Keisha who was already shaking her head. "Why are you shaking your head no?"

"Because, I'm not going to the hospital with you."

"If you don't go with me tonight, you can always go in the morning or on Sunday." Darlene walked over to the coat rack and put on her brown leather jacket with the matching gloves.

"Maybe you're not understanding me. I'm not going to the hospital to see him tonight, tomorrow, or ever if I have anything to do with it!"

"So you don't plan on visiting your uncle at all?"

"Nope. It's bad enough I'm here when I really don't wanna be and now you expect me to see him too? I'm fine right here, auntie. After all, I told you I was coming home to visit you."

Darlene threw her hands up not knowing what else to say. "Alright Keisha. I'm leaving. I'll be back in a few hours. If you need me just call."

She nodded her head as her aunt walked out through the side door and left.

She knew when she initially agreed to come home, Darlene probably assumed she would run up to the hospital and visit Jessie too but she never had intentions on doing that. Her aunt had tried to place guilt on her for not wanting to see him but they had never gotten along and Keisha didn't see it being any different. She could barely stand the sight of him when he wasn't sick. So, with Darlene out of the house, Keisha felt like she could finally relax. She hadn't been able to since she arrived. She walked into the living room and took a seat on the couch then flipped through several channels in between dosing off but was unable to take a good nap because her eyes kept popping open.

She finally decided to walk upstairs since it was apparent she wouldn't get any shut eye. Keisha walked up the squeaky, wooden, steps to the first room on the left which used to be her brother's room. She opened the door to find that they turned his room into a guest room. Darlene had it set up like it was straight out of a hotel. It was so nice she could barely remember what Alonzo's room used to look like.

Keisha continued walking and peeked into the next door where Kennedi's room used to be. She found her old room was now an office. Then, she skipped over her aunt's bedroom and the bathroom to the last door at the end which used to be her bedroom.

When she turned the knob to open the door, Keisha found her room to be the most intact out of the three. She was surprised to see some of the things she had left the day she went to college were still there. She picked up a picture of the three of them that was taken the day they first moved in with Darlene and Jessie. She sat the picture back down and went over to her old closet. She turned the gold handle and noticed it was completely full of boxes. Her eyes scanned them until she reached the top one which had "Keisha" written in black marker on it.

Keisha pushed the box to test its heaviness and, when she realized she could lift it, she picked it up. She placed the medium sized parcel on the bed, opened it up, and started to explore its contents. She smiled as she started seeing things that she used to have in her room. Her gray and black boom box she used to blast all the music she wasn't allowed to listen to. She pulled out an old photo album her mother kept when they lived in Youngstown. She picked up a few Word Up! Magazines and a few pieces of clothing Keisha couldn't fit anymore. But, once she moved the garments out of the way she saw something else that struck a cord.

She picked up the black and white composition notebook that looked like all the other ones she used while in school but this one was different. As she brought it closer, she realized this was the journal she kept while she lived there. Her fingers traced over the word "Diary" that she remembered outlining over and over upon occasion.

Keisha clutched the tattered notebook in her hands. She couldn't believe it hadn't been destroyed. Once she left for college, she thought she had included it in with her things but, shortly after she unpacked, she figured out she'd left it along with a couple of things. She thought about coming back home to get it but she was so determined not to come home at all for anything. She figured Jessie would destroy it along with the rest of her things. She started thumbing through a few pages in the beginning when she heard Darlene coming up the steps calling her name. She hurried up and placed her diary underneath her. She sat on it just in time.

"For a minute I didn't know where you were," Darlene said. Keisha glanced down at her watch and had to do a double take. Darlene had been gone for almost three hours but it felt like she'd only been gone twenty minutes.

"Yeah, I've been upstairs looking at all our old rooms. Alonzo's really looks different."

"I decided to make that our guest bedroom just in case one of y'all decided to come home for a visit. I wanted to change yours into my own personal prayer and meditation room but Jessie insisted we didn't need to do anything to this room. He said it was just fine the way it is."

Keisha quickly rolled her eyes. Now why doesn't that surprise me? It doesn't surprise me at all. That man would do any and everything he can just to spite me. That's why I can't stand him now.

"Since you'll be staying the night, you can sleep in the guest room," Darlene replied.

"I'm not staying the night, Darlene. I have a hotel room and that's where I'm about to go. I'm going home in the morning."

"You don't really have to stay at a hotel. We have more than enough room here."

"It's cool. I already have reservations anyway so I think I'll get ready and go there." Keisha got up and picked up the notebook and the old photo album she tried to hide. Darlene, who was already so worked up, she hadn't noticed it at all. Keisha stood up and made her way back downstairs to grab her coat.

"Thanks for the food. And, since I'm leaving in the morning, I probably won't see you before I go so I guess I'll see you whenever," Keisha said as she put on her coat and gave Darlene a hug. She opened up the screen door and walked to her car before her aunt had a chance to say anything else. As far as she was concerned, her mission had been accomplished and her aunt should be satisfied she even came. Keisha was anxious to leave so she could get to her hotel. Even though she had only been in town for a few hours, she was already growing tired of it.

She sat her purse and her things down on the passenger's seat and waved goodbye to her aunt who didn't seem happy at all. She put her seatbelt on and stuck the key in the ignition but her car wouldn't start. She didn't think anything of it because it never gave her any trouble before. She waited about a minute before she stuck the key back in and attempted to start it up again but nothing happened. She figured it just needed a few minutes to sit before she tried again. She decided to wait a few more minutes and attempted a third time until she realized it wasn't gong to start at all. Keisha turned the car off and walked back in the house to join her aunt. It looked like she would be staying there after all.

# chapter 5

"" I got your message the other day. You said you finally went home for a visit this past weekend. I think that's where we'll start," Dr. Karen said as she leaned back in her chair and gave Keisha the cue to speak.

"My aunt's been calling me non-stop for the past few weeks. I've been dodging her. Eventually, I decided to go see her so she'll stop nagging me."

"Okay. So what happened when you got there? How did your visit go?" Karen asked as she jotted a few notes while Keisha continued.

"My visit was okay. I really didn't want to be there in the first place and everything was fine until my aunt thought I was going with her to the hospital to visit Jessie."

"Why didn't you go with her?"

"Because I can't stand Jessie. I have no desire to see him at all. Period."

"And, why don't you want to see him?"

"Honestly, Dr. Karen, I hate him. And right now, his being in the hospital sick like he is hanging on by the skin of his teeth puts a smile on my face." Keisha knew she sounded coldhearted but she figured at least she was being honest.

"So what else happened after that?"

"Well she went to visit my uncle and I stayed at the house until she got back. I tried to leave and stay at a hotel but my car got stuck in her driveway and I couldn't go anywhere so I was forced to stay there. My uncle tried calling to get me to come and visit but I wasn't having it at all. I can't stand that man." Keisha replied and rolled her eyes.

"Now, we're getting somewhere. Let's explore those feelings right there. Why do you feel such hate and disgust when you talk about Jessie?" Karen asked as Keisha shrugged her shoulders.

"I hate him because he has caused me so much pain in my life. I feel like he deserves everything that's coming to him. While I was at my aunt's I found this." Keisha pulled the notebook out of her red leather Coach purse and handed it to her.

"What is it Keisha?" Karen said as she examined the book and flipped through several pages.

"It's my diary. I used to keep when I lived there," she replied.

"Have you read any of it all?"

"No, other than turning a few of the beginning pages, I haven't looked at it." Keisha crossed her arms.

"How long does this journal cover? Do you remember?"

"Yeah, I remember. I started writing in it shortly after my mother died. I was like twelve or thirteen and I wrote in it to the time I left to go college."

"Okay, so here's what I want you to do. I want you to start going through this journal and start reading the entries you wrote then bring it with you when you come for your sessions."

"Karen, I don't know if I really want to read my journal," Keisha said.

"Why? Explain."

"Because there are some things in there that I would rather not read." Keisha placed the notebook back inside of her purse.

"I understand there are a lot of things you don't want to talk about but those are the very things we need to revisit, with your permission, so we can get to the bottom of this." Karen looked into her eyes as she explained. A tear began to run down Keisha's face as she looked away. She didn't want to cry when talking to Dr. Karen but it felt as if she had no control over emotions.

"Look, Keisha, I know this is not going to be easy but I'm here to help you," Karen said as she grabbed Keisha's hand and held onto it. Keisha pulled a tissue out of her pocket.

"Thank you," she answered in between tears.

"And, we're going to take this one step at a time. The only way for you to heal is to go back to the past. That's what I'm here to help you do. We're going to do this together."

# pretty skeletons

As Dr. Karen ended their session, Keisha couldn't stop crying. She knew by agreeing to put herself in treatment she was going to have to get down and personal into the many secrets she'd tried her hardest to forget about. This was the very thing that made her reluctant to seek treatment in the past. Keisha was also aware of the fact they would have to revisit some very ugly things she'd been exposed to and there was a part of her willing to do it but another was scared she might not be strong enough to travel back in time.

David called Keisha during her drive home and said he brought them lunch so they could spend time together so she spent the entire drive to his shop trying to get her face back to normal. She cried so hard her eyes were puffy and red while her entire face appeared to be the color of an apple. Since her skin was normally caramel, it was hard for her to conceal that she'd been crying but she honestly hoped he was too busy to notice.

Keisha pulled into the parking lot of Fresh Line Cutz and checked her appearance in the mirror while she parked in her usual spot right next to her husband's truck. She wasn't totally convinced her face looked one hundred percent better but it was a definite improvement since she left Dr. Karen's office.

She reached in the glove compartment and pulled out a bottle of Visine. She tilted her head back and allowed a few drops to fall in each eye and then she reapplied her lip gloss before she walked in the shop. From the moment she stepped in the door, the customers and others barbers all said hello and complimented her beauty, which always irritated David. It's why they did it anyway.

Her husband let a few comments and stares slide until he had enough.

"Alright yall, that's enough!" David warned as the guys started laughing. Keisha walked up to him and planted a kiss on his lips. David set his clippers down and took his wife by the hand. He led her back, where his office was, and shut the door behind them.

"The guys are little rowdy today, huh?" Keisha laughed and sat next to him on the loveseat.

"Yeah but they better watch it before I fire somebody today. Naw seriously, they only do that because I act irritated but I don't care about them because you're my woman," David smiled and leaned in to meet his wife's succulent glossed up lips.

"Yes I am, baby," Keisha replied and then started looking through the bags of food David bought. Keisha started talking about her day but he interrupted her.

"Have you been crying babe?" David asked as he stared in her face. She hoped he wouldn't notice but, the more she thought about it, she knew he would because David paid that much attention to her and picked up on the smallest things.

"I haven't been crying. Why would you say that?"

"No reason but your face looks a little red. It just looks like you've been crying, that's all."

"I'm fine baby. How has your day been going so far?" Keisha asked, trying to shift the conversation in another direction. She knew her husband showed concern for her but she wanted to discuss what was going on with him.

"Busy! You know everyone trying to come and get a fresh line up and cut for the holiday season so we've been staying busy."

"That's good. I'm happy business is so good especially since there are many shops closing or going bankrupt."

"I know what you're saying. I thank God everyday because I see everyone's businesses in turmoil and I know it's nothing but the Lord that's keeping it all together," David replied.

"You say that but I believe you continue to excel in your business because you're a very hard worker and a good man."

"Yeah, and that's true too but you know I have to give God his just due. I wouldn't have this shop if it wasn't for him," David explained while Keisha could feel an attitude rising up within her. She knew off top David was a super spiritual man who had a very active Christian life and, while that didn't bother her, she didn't want any parts of it.

Most of the time, Keisha found herself agreeing with him just to prevent any further lectures. She really didn't believe in God and hadn't believed in him since she was a little girl. Once she grew older, she didn't plan on believing in Him again. Most people would call her an Atheist but she felt that was too strong of a word to identify her religious belief. She didn't refer to what she believed in such a rigid tone. Rather, she didn't care to concern herself with the things concerning God at all. She respected her husband and what he chose to put his faith in but that's pretty much where it ended for her.

Keisha took a deep breath. "You know what honey, you're right."

"Are you sure you're okay?"

"Yeah, I'm fine."

"Since you've come back from Columbus you've been acting different," David said as Keisha shook her head in protest.

"Stop worrying baby, I'm fine. You know how my family can stress me out but it's all good. Everything is gonna be fine." David's alarm sounded on his Blackberry and he pressed the button to silence it.

"Oh yeah, that reminds me. The twins are in the Christmas program tonight and, since I'll be working a little later than usual today, I need for you to get them ready and take them to church. I'll meet you there."

"What time does the program start?" Keisha asked as she looked down at her watch.

"Six."

"You'll be done in enough time. I'll get them ready and you can swing by and grab them for church," Keisha reasoned. She tried to avoid church at any costs. It wasn't her favorite place at all and the only time she seemed to go is if David begged her to come or the kids were involving in something.

David glanced at the clock on his phone then said, "Keisha, my last appointment is at six. I'll be lucky to make it to church by seven. I still have to come home, shower, and get dressed too."

"Alright fine. I'll take the kids." Keisha answered not knowing what else to say. David leaned in and kissed his wife on the cheek then they sat and ate their lunch together.

Keisha picked the kids up from school on her way home and, when they got there, she let them play while she cooked dinner. As the chicken baked in the oven, she opened up her purse and pulled the notebook out. She placed it on the dining room table and stared at it for five minutes before finally opening it to read the first entry.

*Dear Diary,*

*I'm new to this diary thing but I've decided to write regardless. I've never kept a diary until now but, before we left our old neighborhood to move with Darlene and Jessie, it was given to me by Ms. Gina. She said it would probably be a good idea to write down how I was feeling and my thoughts and, while I'm not sure why I'm doing this, she claims it will help me. Who knows what it will do but I guess it won't hurt. We've been living with Darlene and Jessie for about a month now and it's cool for the most part. They have us living in this big house in a neighborhood with absolutely no Black people and everything we could ever want but I still miss Youngstown. That's where home is to me. Even though we were living in the hood and our mother was on drugs, we were still all together and a real family. Now, we live with two people that I never knew existed. My aunt Darlene swears up and down that she used to live near us when Alonzo and I were younger but I don't remember her at all and neither does Alonzo. Anyway the way they live their lives and the life we're used to are two different things. We're in church every time we blink (I wish I was exaggerating) and they insist on us dressing up and sitting on the first row right along with them. I've never been to church in my life and I don't know if I like it just yet but I have no choice because that's one of their rules. I have to go. Seems like they have a gazillion rules too. Overall, life with Darlene and Jessie is cool. Alonzo and Kennedi are doing good too. Alonzo's not used to someone telling him what to do but he'll get used to it and Kennedi is really having the time of her life. They give her whatever she wants and she feels like she's the queen of the world. We are all doing good here in Columbus but what I wish most of all was that Mommy was here to see it all.*

*Keesh*

"Mommy, is something burning?" Katrina asked as she ran into the kitchen snapping Keisha back into the present. Keisha set the notebook down and rushed over to the stove and pulled down the oven door. She checked her chicken which seemed to be fine but realized her macaroni and cheese did burn.

She turned the eye underneath the pot off and took it to the sink. She was so engrossed in her diary she didn't even notice the noodles overcooking.

"Thank you, honey. You've saved the day. Now make sure you and your brother grab your coats and meet me back down here because we're about to leave."

"Okay mommy!" Katrina gave her mom a hug and started running up the steps calling her brother's name.

"Don't forget your Christmas speech papers. They're upstairs too," Keisha reminded them and turned the stove off at the same time. She had been so caught up with her diary that she didn't even realize that time had slipped away from them and if they didn't leave now they would be late for the Christmas program. She decided to put the chicken in the fridge for another day but had to pitch everything else. She opened up the lid on the trash can and the contents of her burnt dinner inside. Besides she could always order pizza for them to eat once they returned home from church.

# chapter 6

The parking lot at New Word Christian Center was packed to capacity, regardless to its ability to hold almost five hundred cars. There were barely any spots left so Keisha drove around it twice before she found one. That was another reason why she didn't like coming to church. They were always inviting people but, when you actually attended, there's absolutely no room for you.

Once she and the children made it inside, she noticed twice as many people than cars outside and honestly hoped the Christmas program didn't last too long because she didn't feel like being bothered with all those people. Besides, she didn't even know most of them and would rather be at home relaxing as opposed to being stuck in church anyway.

"Hey Kennedi. I didn't expect you to be here," Keisha said as she ran into her sister in the lobby. She looked like a complete mess, as usual.

"David invited me the other day. You know I was coming to see my niece and nephew. And, Quincy loves to come to church. I should bring him more often."

"It's packed in here today," Keisha said as she looked around at all of the people cluttering the lobby and surrounding hallways.

"It sure is. That's why I'm glad I came early and got me a seat."

"Did you happen to save me one?" Keisha asked. She didn't want to have to stand up during the program.

"Yeah, I actually saved a couple. I saved you, David, and Alonzo a seat."

"Alonzo's coming? How did that happen?" Keisha asked in disbelief. If there was anyone who didn't care for going to church more than her, it was her brother Alonzo. Yet, even though he didn't go to church much, he still claimed to have a personal relationship with Jesus Christ and believed one didn't have stay glued to the pew to be a Christian. Keisha didn't want a relationship with God at all.

"I called him and he said he was coming. And to save him a seat."

"Okay," Keisha answered as D.J. tugged the end of her shirt.

"Mommy, that's our Sunday school teacher right there. We have to go with her." He pointed at the thin dark skinned woman with a short haircut, who stood in the hallway smiling and motioning for them to join her. Keisha nodded her head in approval and the children darted across the lobby.

Keisha followed Kennedi into the sanctuary, to their seats, and they sat down right before the program started. Keisha's eyes scanned the room in search of her mother or father-in-law and, after about five minutes, she located them sitting across the room a couple of rows up from them.

Kennedi didn't waste anytime trying to be nosey. "So how was your trip home to see Darlene?" she asked while helping her sister remove her jacket. Keisha then set it in the empty seat next to Kennedi.

"Absolutely horrible. I only stayed overnight and then I got in the car and came back home," Keisha replied.

"Did you make it to the hospital to see Jessie?"

"Now you know I didn't go and see that fool. I don't know why you're trying to act like you don't already know what happened because I know you talk to Aunt Darlene on a constant basis. She told me..." Keisha tried to remain at a whisper but her voice rose slightly as she finished her statement. Before Kennedi could open her mouth and make up a lie, the children took the stage and it wasn't too long before Katrina and D.J. made their way to stand on the platform with the others.

Keisha smiled at her children as they swayed back and forth singing O Come All Ye Faithful. It made her quite happy to see her children having the time of their lives with not a care in the world, which is how they should be. They did exactly what they were supposed to be doing – enjoying their childhood. She began to think back to when she had that feeling and the only time she remembered experiencing even an inkling of normalcy was when her mother was alive. She felt like, after her mother died, so did her life as she knew it. That's why she prided herself in being able to give her children what she never had. At least, they would never know the personal torment and anguish she faced on a daily basis and Keisha didn't care what lengths she had to go through to make sure it stayed that way.

"Keisha you cool? Looks like you're thinking about something," Kennedi said forcing Keisha to come back to the present moment. She shook her head several times and glanced up at the stage. She didn't even know her mind had drifted off so quickly but, lately, it seemed like it drifted a lot faster than usual.

"I'm fine sis. Was just thinking about something that happened earlier," Keisha answered.

"Oh, there's David. He just walked in the door," Kennedi said as she raised her hand so he could see them. Right as he sat down, Katrina and D.J. stepped in front of the other children and started reciting their speech. Keisha grinned from ear to ear as she watched her daughter repeat her parts verbatim like she read from piece of a paper. David stood up and snapped a few pictures and then sat down.

For once Keisha was glad she actually came, even if it was only to support them.

"They did so good," David said as the twins spotted him and waved at him.

"They sure did! Those are my babies," Keisha exclaimed.

At the end of the program, one of the ministers announced that there would be refreshments in the fellowship hall but everyone seemed to linger around in the sanctuary to socialize with each other.

"Hey daughter! It's so good to see you," a voice called from behind Keisha.

"Hey mom, I'm happy to see you too. You look so nice today. I'm loving your new cut," Keisha complimented her mother-in-law, Cecilia on her brand new style. Cecilia smiled as she ran her hand down her hair. "You know me. I wanted to try something different."

"Well you should've kept it the same. Cutting all of my long hair," John replied as he walked up to where they stood to join the conversation.

"Oh, you'll be alright honey. I just cut it into a bob. You act like I shaved my head bald," Cecilia said but John acted as though he was pouting.

"You might as well have. Hey baby," John replied and gave Keisha a big hug.

"Hey dad. You're sad about Cecilia's hairstyle. I think it's cute on her," Keisha smiled at her mother-in-law.

"I knew you would take her side. But, I know my son agrees with me. Don't you son?"

"Dad, you know I usually am on your side with a lot of things but mom's hair does look nice." David bent his six foot four frame down and kissed her.

"Thank you, son."

"I guess I'm outnumbered. Let me go and hug the only two people I have left on my side." John pointed over to Katrina and D.J. and walked in their direction.

"Your father is too funny," Keisha laughed.

"I don't know why he has this thing about mom cutting her hair."

"Oh my goodness, how long has he been like that?" Kennedi asked.

"Since we got married. He's a firm believer that a woman's hair is her glory but my argument is I'm the one stuck with doing it, so I feel how I wear it is up to me."

"You got that right, mom. He'll get over it," Keisha said. Cecilia signaled for John's attention from across the room and mouthed something to him as if they were conversing in a foreign language.

"He better get over it, if he wants some tonight!" She slapped hands with Keisha and Kennedi. David plugged his ears.

"Okay Ma, that's too much information. I really didn't need to hear that."

"No it isn't, David. Don't act like you don't know. Your two kids didn't just magically appear. You know exactly what time it is."

"Alright Ma!" David replied in attempt to silence her. He wasn't trying to hear anything else pertaining to her sexual relations with his own father.

"Okay everyone. I'll see you all later on this week for Christmas dinner." Cecilia walked off, grabbed John by his arm and they both exited the sanctuary together.

"Baby, your parents are so in love!" Keisha smiled at David. Kennedi's phone began to sound off with Ray J's Sexy Can I ringtone, and Keisha laughed as her sister scrambled to answer it. She stepped away from where they stood to take the phone call. While her sister was on her phone, Keisha's cell vibrated and she picked it up to see a text message from Darlene.--

I was very disappointed you didn't come to see me while you were here in town. You know I wanted to see you. That's why I asked Darlene to get you to come home. I hope to lay my eyes on you very soon. Jessie.

Keisha rolled her eyes as she read the message again and, since she was at church, decided to toss her phone back in her purse rather than throw it across the room.

"Honey, my parents make me sick sometimes," David said as she hit his arm playfully. Just as she got ready to tell him what she made for dinner, Keisha was interrupted by Kennedi and the phone conversation she held on the side. Keisha didn't have a clue as to who her sister talked to but whoever it was had her sister pacing back and forth in a nervous pattern. Keisha walked up to Kennedi and touched her arm.

"What's wrong sis? What's going on?" She asked as her sister began to cry.

"Keisha, it's Alonzo. We gotta get to the hospital. He's been beat up pretty bad."

"What?" Keisha asked in disbelief as her sister broke down upon the revelation. Kennedi embraced Keisha then managed to raise her voice just above a whisper and uttered, "He might not make it."

"Let's go!" David said as he too overheard the conversation.

Keisha was thankful her husband decided to drive them to the hospital because she knew she wasn't in the proper state of mind to do it herself. And, if left up to her sister, they would be on the side of the road somewhere dead. Kennedi could barely drive when all is good so she definitely didn't entrust her life to her under the circumstances. On the drive to the Summa Health Care, David and Kennedi took turns praying for faith and intervention but, as Keisha stared out the window, she secretly wished they'd both shut up. She understood her husband had a strong relationship with God and her sister believed too but she felt like it wasn't the time or the place to be calling on Him. He always seemed to be absent when he was needed the most, in her mind. There was actually a point in time when she was a Christian and went to church frequently. She used to read her Bible and could pray better than anyone with a telecast on television but those days were long gone as far as Keisha was concerned. Besides, she felt like if God wanted to help them he wouldn't have allowed such a horrible thing to happen to her brother or her for that matter. When they pulled into the hospital's parking deck, Keisha could do nothing but shake her head back and forth, crying. However, she did pull herself together enough to jump out of the car and hurry inside along with David and her sister.

"Can you please tell me what room Alonzo Stewart is in?" Kennedi asked the E.R. desk attendant as she signed in. The attendant, already on the phone with someone else, placed the caller on hold and flipped through some papers. The strawberry blonde woman told them the floor and room.

"Thank you ma'am," David replied and followed Keisha to the elevator. Keisha placed her hands on her chest as they rose to the fifth floor intensive care unit. Her heart palpitated as if it struggled to stay in her chest. She closed her eyes momentarily until a noise sounded, causing the door to slide open.

A security guard stood outside the ICU and pointed in the direction of Alonzo's room. As they approached it, a nurse stopped them.

"Are you Mr. Stewart's family?"

"Yes. We're his sisters," Keisha announced as she crossed her arms over her chest, hoping to steady her irregular heartbeat.

# pretty skeletons

"Your brother is in a critical state right now. We're working hard to stabilize him and he seems to be responding well to our interventions."

"So what does that mean exactly?" Kennedi asked.

"He's not stable as of yet but he's improved since he arrived. You can go and see him. But, I must warn you he was beat pretty badly and he's still sedated so he probably won't respond but you can still talk to him anyway," she explained as she closed the medical chart shut.

"Thank you," Keisha and Kennedi replied in unison. Before the nurse walked away, she pulled them to the side.
"Do you have any idea who would've done something like this to your brother?" She looked at them for at least a clue or something that could've explained the severity of Alonzo injuries.

"I wish we could tell you something but we don't know anything ourselves," Keisha answered.

"Okay, well if you hear anything make sure you contact the detective on this card. He was here earlier checking on your brother and will be the one trying to find out who did this." The nurse handed it to Keisha. She placed the card inside of her purse and turned around to face the door of Alonzo's room. She stood outside as if her feet were cemented to the floor with glue. Her sister nudged her and said, "Let's go in and see him."

She nodded and followed behind her baby sister. She could hear machines beeping as she entered the room, sounding off as if they were creating a rhythm. At the same time, she could feel her heart beat picking up at an incredulous pace.

"Oh my God! Oh..." Kennedi said as she let go of Keisha's hand to cover her mouth.

"Alonzo?" Keisha said as she began to cry. A wave of sadness swept over her while she stared at her brother lying on the hospital bed. There were various tubes sticking out of everywhere. One even came from his mouth, figured to be the respirator helping him to breathe. His face was so swollen and cut up he was unrecognizable. Keisha walked in closer and touched her brother's hand. She began to wonder who could do such a crazy thing to another person. Her thoughts took her back to their last conversation and how Alonzo asked for a ridiculous amount of money. She immediately felt, by looking at him, his condition was a result of his failure to secure the money.

She clutched her brother's hand tighter as she wept. David came from behind and put his arms around her. She remembered seeing Alonzo a couple of days prior while watching him hang on for dear life. This whole scenario didn't seem real or fair. Keisha had always believed life dealt her a losing hand and didn't know why she expected it to be any different.

"I need to get some fresh air for a bit." Keisha let go of her husband's embrace.

"You need me to walk with you baby?" David asked in a sincere tone of voice.

"No, I think I need to be by myself," she whispered fighting back another string of tears that were threatening to escape her tear ducts.

"I'm going to stay with Alonzo, Keisha," Kennedi replied and Keisha nodded while making her way through the room and out the door. She was glad her sister decided to stay with David because she definitely needed to be alone and collect her thoughts.

She walked to the elevator and took it down to the basement where the cafeteria was located. Once she entered the food court, she noticed there were only a few people scattered throughout the open space. Keisha ordered a coffee then found a spot in a secluded corner and sat down.

Her hands trembled as she lifted the cup to her mouth. Her usual composed demeanor had been replaced with a nervousness she couldn't shake. With each sip, she thought about the possibility of her brother not making it and that notion alone made her sick to her stomach.

"So… I see time hasn't changed you one bit. You're still beautiful," a man from behind said. For a split second, she didn't know who spoke to her but, as the sound penetrated her auditory senses, she recognized the familiar voice.

"Malik?" Keisha replied. She stood up, turned around, and stood face to face with Malik Harris, the one man from her past who knew a little too much about her and the very one she thought she'd left where her past was physically located… in Columbus. It had been such a long time since she'd seen Malik and so much had taken place since then. When they lived in Columbus, he used to be best friends with Alonzo and was nothing but trouble. But, even though he lived life dangerously and by his own rules, it didn't stop Keisha from being in a relationship with him. So, just seeing him standing before her brought back some memories she didn't even want to recall. The sight of him in her presence made her skin crawl as well.

"What are you doing here?" Keisha asked as she looked around nervously.

"Don't act happy to see me," Malik said as he looked her up and down as if she were a piece of Angus beef. He licked his lips in one swift motion indicating to Keisha that he liked what he saw but she ignored his advances.

"I'm sorry. I didn't mean to say it like that but I'm just surprised to see you. That's all."

"Oh, it's okay. I did walk up on you without warning."

"I'm definitely shocked."

"So, what's good with Keisha Sheridan?"

"It's Keisha Mahone. I'm married," she lifted up the three carat diamond-studded princess cut ring and diamond wedding band that adorned her left ring finger so he could check out her "bling" up close and personal. He smiled then allowed a cocky chuckle to escape from his lips.

"Yeah, I know you married. How long?"

"Seven years."

"You've been married for seven years?"

"Yeah, I have."

"It hasn't been that long since the last time I saw you," Malik asked.

"It's been longer than that," Keisha replied.

"Wow, time flies for real!"

"It sure does."

Keisha started to go back down memory lane in her mind to last time she saw him. They were still together and she was more miserable than she'd ever been. She had desperately wanted to leave him and be done with his unstable lifestyle but there was something about him that made it hard for her to let go. He had the type of qualities that made you become addicted to him while she had found herself addicted to both him and the same poison he sold on the street.

The moment her aunt and uncle found out she was on drugs, they sent her off to rehab. Although, they told her siblings she went to stay with some family for the summer. She ended up leaving rehab and getting accepted in to college the year after she graduated so they never knew of her drug use. She had never heard from Malik again.

She snapped out of her transient flashback in the middle of Malik asking her a question.

"What did you ask me?"

"You already saw your brother or are you about to go up there and see him?" he asked.

"Yeah, I just saw him. But, how did you know he was here?" Keisha responded as she raised her eyebrows. It was already odd for her to be running into him when he didn't live in the area then to run into him at the hospital of all places.

"I know he was here because one of the dudes we roll with called and told me what happened. I came as soon as I heard."

"You stay here now or something?"

Malik flashed his sneaky smile that Keisha knew too well. "Yeah I've been here for about four months now."

If Malik has been here for four months, then why did Alonzo not tell me in the first place? She thought.

"Do you know who would do something like this to my brother?"

"Naw Keesh but I'm keeping my ears open to find out. I won't sleep until I know. Look I gotta run but here's my card. If you need me, just call me." Malik reached out and hugged her before disappearing into the hallway.

Keisha stood there and digested his last words to her and she wasn't sure if she believed him. Matter of fact, she didn't believe him at all. Wherever Malik went, his right hand man, trouble, usually followed and she had reason to think the attack on Alonzo was somehow connected to his sudden presence. And with the reappearance of Malik as well as her aunt and uncle in her own life, she feared her secret past was getting ready to resurface and that fact alone terrified her.

# pretty skeletons

She was starting to become increasingly anxious when she thought about the possibility of her past coming back to the surface. She once felt in complete control of her life but slowly she started feeling like that was changing.

# chapter 7

"**S**o how are you feeling today, Keisha?" Dr. Karen asked as she pressed her designer glasses up on the bridge of her nose.

"I don't know how to feel. Things are so messed up and I feel like everything is my fault."

"What's your fault?"

"My brother is in the hospital, all beat up. I feel like he's there because of me," Keisha paused and took a deep breath before continuing. "About a week ago, he came and asked me for a large amount of money. I didn't give it to him and I believe he was beat up as a result of it."

"You think he was injured because of you?" Karen asked and Keisha shook her head.

"Basically, in a nutshell," Keisha stated then stared toward the ceiling. "Everything is always my fault. That's the way it's always been. And, now not only are my aunt and uncle trying their best to be back in my life, I just ran into my ex-boyfriend Malik. I swear I can't catch a break for nothing," Keisha sighed and crossed her arms.

"So I'm assuming he was not someone you wanted to see either," Karen replied while jotting a few things down.

"Not at all Karen. When I left Columbus, he was one of the people along with Darlene and Jessie that I never wanted to see again and now they've reappeared. I'm getting nervous."

"You're getting nervous about what?"

Keisha took in Dr. Karen's question, looked away, and put her head down before she responded, "I'm nervous because there are a lot of things that have happened to me that no one knows about. And, with everything that has taken place in the last few weeks, I have this deep feeling it's about to resurface."

"Do you want to talk about these secrets?"

For a moment, Keisha hesitated. She wanted to open up and tell the doctor all of her innermost secrets but was afraid. Not only was she scared of revealing the depths of her soul, she hadn't told anyone what had happened to her over the course of life, before she met her husband. Kennedi, Alonzo, and David didn't have a clue as to what had gone on in her past – under the custody of Darlene and Jesse. None of them knew what she prepared to reveal to a complete stranger.

"Keisha, I know you're afraid to open up and tell me but that's what I'm here for. I won't ask you to discuss anything you don't want to and we'll move at your pace. So, just tell me what you want to do and we'll go from there."

Keisha didn't answer initially. She deeply exhaled, unzipped her purse, and pulled out her diary.

"In order to understand what I'm saying and how I feel, I have to start from the beginning." Keisha thumbed through the first couple entries then flipped to the page that marked the moments she lost her innocence. She picked up the notebook and started to read aloud.

"My uncle stared at me today. He's looked at me before but today was different. He looked at me in a different way, like how a boy looks at a girl when he likes her. That's exactly how Jessie looked at me. He picked me up from school because I missed the bus and, once we got home and we pulled into the driveway, that's when it all started. I thanked him for picking me up and went to get out of his car when started looking at me strangely. At first, I didn't think anything of it until he continued to stare. He had his eyes stuck on me like he was under some sort of magic spell and didn't stop until I reached the porch. Then, Jessie smiled at me. I want to think it was nothing... but I don't have a good feeling about the way he looked at me."

A single tear rolled down Keisha's caramel colored skin as she shut the notebook and put it back inside her purse. She crossed her arms and rubbed her shoulders as she cried. That was the first time Keisha had read those words since she'd written them and, even though much time had passed since that incident, it still felt as though it happened yesterday - almost as if a dried up, crusty scab had been pulled back to expose the fresh flesh of a wound. She zipped up her purse and attempted to speak but immediately shed tears. Karen closed up her legal pad, "I'll think we'll stop here for today."

Keisha knew that, by going to treatment, her past would begin to be uncovered but she never imagined it to hurt so much. Because she tried hard to bury those bones over the years, she hesitated about proceeding with the treatment process as she didn't want to relive the most painful time in her life. It scared her to revisit that which almost destroyed her.

As she left Dr. Karen's office, she turned her cell phone back on and realized she missed several calls from David. She turned her car on and began to drive off before she called her husband. He answered on the third ring.

"What's up baby? I've been trying to reach you for a while. Where you at?"

"I apologize, babe. My phone was on silent and at the bottom of my purse."

"You get most of your shopping done?" David asked as Keisha got caught by a red light.

"I'm almost done. I have a few more stores to hit and I'll be coming home," she replied.

"Okay, sounds good. Now, I know I keep asking you the same question but is everything okay with you? I know the holidays are a rough time for year."

"Yeah, I'm fine David. Just a little tired but otherwise I'm fine."

"Well, good thing you'll be home soon because I have a few presents I would like to unwrap before Christmas. If you know what I mean!" Keisha smiled as she read between the lines.

"Oh yeah and where are the kids?"

"They're here but they'll be in bed by the time you get home."

"In that case, let me hurry up and run to these stores so I can get home."

Keisha took a trip to the only place where she knew she would be able to find everything all under one roof, Super Wal-Mart. Since it was the day before Christmas, the store was completely packed with customers who had waited until the last minute to complete their shopping. But, she made herself a list before she left home and was on a mission to get out of there as soon as possible.

Forty-five minutes and a slight attitude later, Keisha pushed an overflowing shopping cart out of the store and into the congested lot.

"Where in the world did I park?" Keisha said aloud as she stared at the sea of cars, trying to locate her car. It didn't take her too long to figure out where it was and when she finally reached it, she popped her trunk. While wishing David was there to help her, she began to load her car up with shopping bags when she felt someone approaching her from behind. She turned around.

"So we keep bumping into each other. I think it must be fate," Malik smiled. Keisha rolled her eyes and smacked her lips.

"You may think it's fate but I think you're following me," she continued to load up her trunk.

"I'm not following you. I just closed up my salon across the street and had to run in and grab a few things from Wal-Mart, so I'm hardly following you."

"What salon do you have?" Keisha asked as she put her hands on her hips.

"Platinum Style."

"That's your salon?"

"It sure is. I just opened it a few months ago."

"Yeah, I remember when it opened," Keisha said as she stared at Malik.

"Why are you looking at me like that? I mean I know I'm fine but..." he replied and acted as though he was adjusting his clothes. Keisha shook her head and laughed at him.

"You're still cocky too. You haven't changed at all," Keisha stated as Malik handed her a bag of potatoes.

"I wouldn't be Malik if I wasn't cocky."

"I forgot."

"So where's your husband at? He'll probably flip if he comes out the store and see you talking to me." Malik looked around as if he was nervous but Keisha wasn't fooled at all. He was never the type of person to be scared of anyone and she was certain he definitely hadn't changed.

"My husband's not here. He's at home. I just came out to finish up some last minute shopping."

"Let me ask you sumthin.' Are you really married? Every time I've seen you, he's missing in action." He placed the last bag in the trunk and shut it closed. Keisha picked up her hand and flashed her ring.

"Yes Malik, I'm married. What you think I brought this big rock for myself?"

Malik shrugged his shoulder. "I don't know. Anything's possible nowadays."

"Whatever man. I am married and that's all you need to know."

"Excuse me, Miss Thang. Or, should I say Mrs. Thang! I see you haven't lost that smart mouth of yours."

"I sure haven't," Keisha replied as she looked down at her cell phone and noticed she had a message from David. I can't wait til you get home. Keisha smiled as she read between the lines. She figured he had something up his sleeve and was totally game for whatever he had in store. Malik noticed Keisha smiling and giggling for what seemed like no reason at all.

"Did I say something funny?" he asked as he watched her cheeks blush.

She cleared her throat, "It's nothing Malik. I was just thinking about something. But look, I do have to run so I guess I'll see you around." She tucked her phone back into its case and started walking away but he called her name again to stop her.

"So you're gonna leave just like that?"

"What do you mean?" Keisha asked with a confused look on her face. She didn't have a clue as to what he hinted at.

"You're just gonna leave without giving me your number?" he asked as he held up his hands.

"Yeah. Why do you need my number, Malik? I'm married or have you forgotten already?"

"I need your number because I want to keep in touch with you. But, you think I have another agenda and it's not even like that. I just want to stay in touch."

"You wanna keep up with me?"

"Of course. That is if you're allowed to give out your phone number. I wouldn't want to make hubby mad."

"Now, you're trippin'… I don't have to ask permission to give out my number. Give me your phone," Keisha said as she snatched it out of his hands. Malik smiled as she programmed her cell number into his address book and she gave it back to him.

"Oh before I forget have you found out anything about the guys who beat up Alonzo?" Keisha asked. Malik shook his head no.

"Naw, baby girl. I'm still investigating that myself and I won't sleep until I find some answers" he replied as he winked at her.

"See you around, Malik," she smiled then got in her car and drove off.

She glanced in her rearview mirror and looked at Malik as he watched her drive away with a huge smile on his face. She couldn't help but wonder what he thought in that busy mind of his but she hoped it didn't concern her at all. She honestly shouldn't have given him her number but figured he probably wouldn't call her anytime soon so she really had nothing to worry about. Her phone began to ring interrupting her thoughts about Malik.

"Hello?" Keisha answered without even looking at caller ID which she usually did.

"Hey Keisha, baby. It's me, your Uncle Jessie."
Keisha almost swerved off the side of the road when she heard his voice. He didn't have to announce himself because he was the only one who ever called her "Keisha Baby" – the term of endearment he'd created for her that she absolutely loathed.

"I know who it is. Why are you calling me?" she asked as she pulled into the housing development where she resided.

"I can't believe you're still mad at me. We haven't talked in years. Why can't we just let the past be the past and move on?" Jessie said as she could feel her heart beating fast.

"Can you take back and erase all the stuff you've done to me?"

# pretty skeletons

"Come on, you know I can't do that. That's a rhetorical question."

"Well then, you definitely have your answer. I don't have anything to say to you and you definitely don't have anything to say to me. So, just let me live my life and leave it at that," Keisha replied but, before she could hang up, Jessie spoke.

"But, I need to talk to you."

She pressed the end button stopping him from continuing to say anything else to her. She couldn't believe he had the audacity to call her when she told him she never wanted to see or talk to him again. The day she left for college, she thought she made herself very clear. And, when she'd gone to visit her aunt, she thought she'd reiterated her point but see he didn't get the hint just like Darlene failed to do.

By the time she parked her car in the garage, she was steaming mad. Her nostrils flared and her chest rose and fell harshly. From the moment, her husband saw her he knew something was wrong.

"Keisha what's going on?"

"Nothing David. I really don't even wanna talk about it." Keisha hung up her coat in the hall closet and then noticed the dining room was set up for what would've been a romantic evening between them. She was previously in the mood but, after Jessie's pop up phone call, she didn't want any parts of it.

David came behind her and began to rub her shoulders. His strong hands did help to ease the tension she felt rising up in her back but didn't help her attitude at all.

"Well, I don't want you to focus on anything else right now. Let's enjoy this beautiful dinner I've cooked just for you and all of the surprises I have planned after dessert," David explained and then planted soft, sweet kisses on her neck. His hands began to move further down her curvaceous body as he attempted to rub all her worries and stress away. Keisha found herself succumbing to his advances and took a step forward to separate herself from his embrace.

"Baby, I know you've gone to a lot of trouble preparing this special dinner for me but I'm just not in the mood." Keisha slid out of her shoes and placed them by the door.

"Come one baby, let's have dinner and I promise I'll help you to relax." David started to wrap his arms around her but she pulled away.

"I'm so sorry, bay, but I think I need to go and lay down," she replied as she went upstairs to their master bedroom. Keisha knew she was wrong for standing David up on the romantic dinner but hadn't planned on Jessie calling out of the blue. She couldn't understand why he insisted on talking to her after she asked him to leave her alone. Hearing Jessie's voice changed her entire mood and all she wanted to do was go to sleep and forget he ever called her. She actually desired to erase his total existence from her memories but knew that wasn't going to happen at all. As she climbed in bed, she tried to relax and put the phone call out of her mind but it was the only thing she could think about. She knew she had another sleepless night ahead of her.

"Merry Christmas!" The twins screamed at the same time causing Keisha jolt from her sleep. Her eyes popped open and she sat up fast, thinking something was wrong with her children until she saw the wide grins across their faces.

"Good morning babies," she said before yawning and then the kids jumped on the bed to join her. She looked over to see David had already gotten up. And, from the looks of his side of the bed, he hadn't occupied his space all night. "Katrina where's daddy at?" Keisha asked as she planted a kiss on their foreheads.

"He's waiting on all of us. We went downstairs to open up our presents but daddy said we have to wake you up first."

"Oh okay," she replied. Then, it hit her. She had forgotten to wrap all of the gifts she'd brought for them and couldn't believe she allowed herself to be so absent minded. She never planned on her uncle calling her out of the blue like that and blamed her forgetfulness on the stupid phone call. Keisha jumped out of bed and, before the twins could follow her any further, she said, "Hold on guys, stay right here. Mommy has some special surprises for you but you have to stay here, in me and your dad's bedroom."

"Yay!" D.J. clapped with excitement.

"And I mean stay here. No peeking." Keisha put on her Victoria Secret silk robe and pink slippers and ran downstairs to her car. David was in the kitchen pulling out some items to cook for breakfast.

"Where ya going, babe?" he asked as he saw Keisha walking past him quickly without even saying a word. "I totally forgot I had all those gifts and groceries in the car and I didn't wrap any of them so I have the kids waiting upstairs in our room while I figure out a plan."

"Babe, don't worry. I have everything under control. I brought all the bags in and wrapped them last night. Just relax." He smiled and she exhaled. She was so glad he went behind her because she felt horrible to think everything was still in the trunk.

"Thank you so much. I appreciate you, baby." Keisha reached out and pulled David into her embrace. She leaned up on her toes and gave him a juicy kiss before she added, "And I'm sorry for ruining last night. I know you went through a lot of trouble to put our romantic dinner together and I messed it all up."

"It's cool, honey. We'll have a chance at another evening like that very soon. I just want you to be alright," David said as he looked his wife in her eyes. She took that moment to kiss him again and smiled.

"Everything is fine. Don't worry at all about me," Keisha replied and honestly felt like kicking herself for not being honest with her husband.

"Babe, are you sure? I can tell when something is wrong with you. You just don't seem yourself" David said as he examined her inconsistent facial expressions. One minute, it seemed as though she was on top of the world. The next, it looked like she was going to break down and cry. Keisha smiled and reassured her husband that she was okay but truthfully the phone call from Jessie threw her completely off track. Being back in contact with the two people that she despised had her emotions running wild and she started feeling like she was losing control. She decided to do the only thing that could help her calm her nerves even if it was only temporary and that was sleep.

"Babe, I honestly think I'm tired from all of the running I've been doing over the holidays. I'll be okay. I think I just need to take a nap and I'll be all rested to go to your mom's in a little while." Keisha explained. David kissed her on her forehead.

"Okay honey. I'll go and feed the kids. Once I get them all together, we can go then."

Keisha smiled, "Sounds like a plan."

Keisha walked up the steps, nestled herself deep in the covers on her bed, and hoped a nap would remedy how she felt at the moment.

As they sat at David's parent's dinner table, preparing for their traditional holiday meal, Keisha was glad she got some rest because she felt much better.

"Lord, I pray that you may add a blessing to this food and that it would nourish our bodies. I pray that you would bless the hands that prepared it in Jesus name. Amen," John said as everyone around the table repeated "Amen" then started to help themselves to the massive spread.

"The food looks delicious mom. You've really out done yourself this year." Keisha smiled at Cecilia as she picked up a plate.

"Thank you, baby. You know I love to cook," she replied and then David decided he wanted to add his two cents.

"Ma, with all this food you've cooked, you would think you were cooking for a small army. We are not going to be able to eat all this."

"I know it is a lot but I couldn't help myself. Once I got in the kitchen and put on my worship music, Jesus took over." Cecilia laughed.

"Well, why don't you call your sister Kennedi and see if she would like to bring her family over and join us," John suggested. "You know what Dad, that's such a good idea, I'll go and call her right now." Keisha excused herself from the table and went into the living room. After she confirmed her sister would indeed join them, she sat down on the couch instead of returning back to the dinner table. She knew the holidays were supposed to be a time of gladness and joy where you find comfort in spending it with the ones you love. And,

# pretty skeletons

even though she enjoyed being around her husband's family, she still felt as though a huge part of her was missing. Keisha missed her mom. She missed her mother's laugh and how it would fill the room when she was tickled about something. She missed the great Christmases they had even when living in the worst part of town. Rita always made sure Santa visited their house. It didn't matter how much money she had in her pocket, she always made sure they had a truck load of presents underneath their Christmas tree. She cried as she began to think of the huge void since the loss of her mother. It had proven to be something no one or nothing could fill. Keisha had even reasoned within herself that it might not ever be filled because, despite losing her mother sixteen years prior, the pain still felt fresh. Rita left here way too soon, she thought.

"Baby, why are you crying?" David said as he approached her. It was too late for her to try to cover up her tears and act like she hadn't been crying.

"I just really miss my mom. You know how I get around this time of the year and, now with everything that has happened to Alonzo, it's not making me feel any better," Keisha said as she reached onto the end table and pulled a tissue out of the box. She dabbed away her tears only to allow a new stream to fall down her face.

"I know this is a hard time for you but I want you to know you don't have to deal with it alone. I'm here to help you through this rough time. I love you," David said as he put his arm around her and pulled her in close to him. In his embrace, she began to sob.

"I love you too and I appreciate you being here for me baby. I'm usually able to handle things a little better than this but I've been thinking about her a lot lately."

"And that's okay, babe. You're human. You're allowed to think about your mom and its okay if you shed some tears. That's normal. You don't have to be superwoman. Let what you're feeling out. We mess up when we try and hold everything inside."

"You're right. Sometimes I forget that."

"When we don't deal with the very thing that continues to bother us, we set ourselves up for disaster because we don't get to the root of the problem. Sometimes, we keep dealing with a certain thing until we learn how to handle it properly. The only way we can move on from what has happened in our past is if we're willing to deal with it."

All Keisha could do was shake her head yes as she rested her head on his chest. She didn't know where this advice came from all of a sudden but he almost sounded like he had a conversation with Dr. Karen. She knew her husband was being truthful and only suggesting those things to help but couldn't help to wonder if she would ever be able to move on beyond all of her painful experiences.

# chapter 8

"Keisha, can you call these lists of clients and reschedule all my appointments to match this schedule right here?" Michael said as he handed her some documents along with his personal calendar.

"Sure, I'll get right on it," she replied as she placed the items on her desk. She expected him to turn right back around and head in the direction of his office but, when he didn't, she looked up and raised her eyebrows.

"Do you need me to do anything else?" Keisha inquired.

"I don't know how to say this and correct me if I'm wrong, but something's different with you. I've noticed it since we've come back from Christmas vacation." He crossed his arms as he awaited her response.

Normally, her boss Michael wasn't one to pry or get involved in anyone's personal business but they had known each other for several years and had become almost like family in the time she'd been employed by him.

Keisha shook her head and reassured him, "I'm fine. Why does it seem like I've been acting funny?"

"You haven't been acting funny. It just seems like something is weighing heavy on your mind that's all. You sure everything okay? How's your brother?"

"Yeah, everything is fine. You gave us so much time off. I'm just trying to get back into the swing of things and Alonzo's doing well. He's home and getting back on his feet." Keisha let out a laugh and flashed the best smile she could muster.

She must've convinced Michael everything was okay with her because he returned the gesture. But truthfully, her brother had been released from the hospital and doing quite well even though the doctors didn't think he would make it but Keisha couldn't be in any worse shape.

From the moment Jessie called her, she hadn't been able to sleep and spent the entire Christmas holiday in a horrible mood. Not only did he call her on Christmas Eve, he took the liberty of calling her every other day since then. Keisha had done everything from hanging up on him, cursing him out, and not returning his phone calls, but he still didn't get the hint. He still called insisting to talk to her and saying how he needed to speak with her in person. He even went on to explain how God led them to meet face to face which led Keisha to stop answering his phone calls altogether. He also had the nerve to call and pray that God would begin to change her callous heart, which only contributed to her increasing frustration with him.

"Okay, Keisha that's great. And I'm sorry if it seems like I'm being nosy but you know I'm just checking. I want you to know if you ever need to talk, I'm here."

"Thanks Michael. I appreciate it," Keisha replied.

"You know what? Why don't you take a long lunch right now and don't worry about doing all of that for me until you get back."

"Are you sure Michael? I can start on this right away if you need me to..."

"No, it's okay. Have a good lunch. You can work on all that later."

Keisha still hadn't agreed to take his offer. She knew that business was typically busy for him during this time of year and, if she didn't start on it soon, work would pile up. She opened up his date book and was about to get started when he stopped her.

"Look, Keisha, I'm still in the Christmas spirit so you better take advantage of this while you can," Michael replied and caused laughter to erupt between them.

"In that case, I'm leaving right now!" Keisha joked before she hurriedly grabbed her keys, purse, and jacket then made a dash for the door. And just as she walked out, she told him thanks.

She was glad he was in a good mood and gave her some extra time for lunch because work was definitely the last thing on her mind. She thought she'd done a great job at putting on a front like everything was fine but she knew her boss could see the evidence of sleepless nights underneath her eyes. Keisha had done her absolute best to cover up the dark circles forming around her hazel almond-shaped eyes but not even MAC makeup could cover up their obvious existence. Lately, it seemed as though everyone around her knew something was wrong with her despite her attempts to assure them they had nothing to worry about. Even when she woke up in the middle of the night in a cold sweat and almost scared David half to death two days prior, she'd managed to convince him it was just a bad dream. She didn't think he totally believed what she had told him but he never pressed the issue any further.

Her cell phone rang and she didn't recognize the number but decided to pick it up anyway.

"Hello?" Keisha answered in her generalized tone, still uncertain of the identity.

"Hey Keisha. What's good?" Malik said in his usual relaxed voice.

"Nothing. On my lunch break. I'm surprised you're calling me."

"Why? I told you I would."

Keisha remembered him saying that but never expected him to call and so soon.

"Yeah. you did. Didn't you?"

"You sound excited to hear from me," Malik replied sarcastically.

"I'm jumping up and down right now."

"Look, I didn't call to argue with you. You did say you're on your lunch break?"

"Yup, I just left my office."

"How about we grab something together? I'm on my lunch too."

"What makes you think that I want to eat with you?" Keisha asked yet Malik laughed at her rudeness.

"Okay then, meet me at Applebee's. I'll be sitting toward the back of the restaurant." Malik didn't even give her a chance to say no. He had already hung up the phone. Keisha laughed, placed her phone down on the passenger's seat, and drove the short distance to meet up with Malik.

Keisha's cell phone rang and she smiled as she heard her husband's ring tone. She had just pulled into the lot of the popular restaurant and decided to park near the back while she conversed with David.

"What's up, baby?" Keisha asked as she put the car in park and shut it off.

"Nothin' babe. I just called to see what you were doing," David answered. She could hear the men from the barbershop carrying on conversation in the background.

"I just left the office and I'm about to grab me some lunch."

"Oh, lunch sounds good. Can you bring me something? I'm starving over here and I've had appointments back to back."

"Honey, I'm sorry. I won't be able to. I have a few errands to run and then it's straight back to work. Michael has a lot of things for me to do at the office."

"It's cool, babe, I'll just get one of my clients to pick me up something. I'll talk to you later."

"Okay. Love you. Bye," Keisha answered as she pressed the end button, shocked she chose to lie to her husband. She couldn't believe she allowed herself to be dishonest when she knew she had more than enough time to get him something and take it to the shop. But she also knew that, if she did, she wouldn't have any time to meet Malik for lunch and had to admit she was curious as to why he'd invite her in the first place.

"Hey Malik. What's up?" Keisha said as he held out a chair for her to sit down.

"You," he answered as he took his seat across from her. A wave of his Kenneth Cole cologne invaded her nostrils and she found herself inhaling the scent she loved to smell on her husband. For a moment, there was an awkward silence residing between them like an unwanted guest. Keisha noticed how he stared at her up and down, checking out the navy blue Donna Karen pantsuit accentuating her best assets. She decided to put an end to it before it went too far.

"So, how you been?" she asked, snapping Malik out of his self-induced trance.

"I've been good. Business has been even better. And you?"

# pretty skeletons

"I've been cool."

"That's what's up. I just left your brother's house. He's doing great too."

"Yeah, his doctor said he should be back to work in the next week or so," Keisha added.

"I'm just glad he's alright. Zoe is like a brother to me and I would've been messed up if something happened to him."

"Me too," Keisha replied as her mind shifted temporarily to the thought of him not being around. Malik noticed the change in her mood and apologized.

"I'm sorry Keesh. I didn't mean to upset you."

"It's okay. I know you didn't mean to. I just feel a bit uneasy knowing that the guys who attacked my brother are still roaming the streets. I talked to the detective briefly the other day and he hasn't heard anything"

"Neither have I. So what did you for New Years?" he asked, completely changing the subject.

"I didn't do anything. My husband took our children to church and I stayed home with my grey goose and watched the ball drop," Keisha replied. Malik looked at her as if he didn't believe what she'd just said.

"Wait a minute. You didn't hit up no parties or the club for the New Year?"

"No, I stayed at the house."

"I can't believe that because the Keisha I used to know would tear the club up every chance she got and was at every party in Columbus."

"Well, that was the Keisha you used to know. I don't party like that anymore. I've changed a lot since then. Besides, my husband isn't into that kind of stuff."

"Oh so you and your husband are holy rollers huh?" Malik laughed and drank some water.

"Man, please. You already know I don't go to nobody's church. God hasn't done anything for me so I'm definitely as far away from the church as I can."

"Here we go! I forgot you used to be the leader of the anti-church revolution."

"Shut up," Keisha laughed. "You know how I feel about the whole subject and it hasn't changed."

# JESSICA A. ROBINSON

"Speaking of which, how are your aunt and uncle?"

Keisha rolled her eyes and sighed before she answered. "Darlene is cool and Jessie just won't leave me alone."

"Y'all still can't get along?"

"We'll never get along," Keisha replied as Malik's attention turned toward someone approaching their table.

"What's up, Miss Kennedi?" Malik asked as she drew closer.

"Nothing at all. I was getting ready to ask you two the same thing," she asked as she looked at her sister straight in her eyes.

"Your sister and I are just out having lunch. Just two friends catching up," Malik answered and flashed his pretty boy smile. Kennedi wasn't impressed or mesmerized at his simple gesture. She smacked her lips and rolled her eyes so hard you would've thought they almost popped out of their sockets.

"Mmm hmm... Well, I gotta run and grab something to eat before my hair appointment but I'll call you later. And it was good seeing you again, Malik," Kennedi said and then walked off.

"I swear Kennedi is feisty just like you," Malik smiled.

"I don't know what her problem is. She's usually in a good mood. Quincy probably did something to make her mad." Keisha's eyes followed her sister as she walked up to the counter, picked up her order, and waved goodbye. She couldn't figure out why her sister acted so funny but made a mental note to text her later.

Malik went to say something but his phone started vibrating on the table.

"I'm sorry but I have to run Keisha! Business calls, but I'll see you around."

"Bye Malik," she answered as he said goodbye and dropped enough money to pay for their lunch and hers for the rest of the week.

Keisha pulled out her phone and texted her sister.

Kennedi, whats up? You were acting funny just now. What's the deal?

Kennedi responded. I should be asking you that. I was pretty surprised to see you and Malik having lunch together.

Keisha replied. Sis, believe me it was nothing. We were just catching up with each other. Nothing less and nothing more.

Kennedi. Ok. If you say so Keisha. Just be careful around Malik. I don't trust him. Never have, never will.

Keisha. I know exactly what you're saying and believe me, it's not that serious.

Kennedi. All I'm sayin' sis is be careful. You know how Malik is.

After Keisha picked up the kids from school, she stopped by the grocery store. By the time her husband made it home by six, she already had lasagna baking in the oven and a garden salad ready on the dinner table. The twins were upstairs watching Dora the Explorer and she had even started whipping up David's favorite dessert, banana pudding.

"Oh my God! It smells heavenly in here." David walked up to Keisha and kissed her on the cheek.

"I guess I was in the cooking mood," Keisha smiled.

"Thank God because I was tired of China Moon, Main Moon, and all those other moons. There isn't nothing like coming home to a home cooked meal by my baby!"

"That's right!" She walked over to the stove and turned off the oven as she looked in on the lasagna.

"I'm glad you're in a better mood. I've been praying for you, honey."

"Yeah, I'm doing better," Keisha replied ignoring his latter statement. David walked up behind her, wrapping his long, muscular arms around her slender frame.

"Babe, I know you've been dealing with a lot and the holidays are a hard time for you but I'm right here to help you through this."

"Thank you." She let out a subtle smile.

"And I've been on my knees, honestly, praying for you and the things you've been through. God has really been speaking to me."

"He has?"

"Yes and I know that church is not your thing but I believe if you start coming with me and the kids, everything will turn around," David reassured. Keisha closed her eyes and laughed before she continued.

"So you believe if I start coming to church then that's supposed to make everything better?"

"Yes babe. I really believe that."

"Well that's what you believe but I don't feel that way."

"Baby, I know you've gone to church in the past. But, have you ever given God a chance?"

"What do you mean? I used to go to church and I believed in God, David, but that was a long time ago. It has nothing to do with my life now!"

"I don't understand. What's so wrong about going to church and believing in God?"

"Because the same people who go to church and claim they believe in God are the same people who are more evil the devil himself!" Keisha covered the banana pudding with aluminum foil and placed the pan inside the refrigerator.

"Why do you feel like that?" David asked as he walked over and tried to embrace her. She pulled away.

"I don't want to talk about it," Keisha replied and started walking up the steps to their master bedroom. She could hear his heavy footsteps behind her. As he stood in the doorway, he didn't say anything. She walked back and forth across the room changing out of her work clothes and into her pajamas. Keisha began to pick up things and set them down for no reason at all.

"Honey, what's wrong? Did I say something that upset you?"

"No, I'm fine," Keisha quickly answered and continued on with what she was doing as if nothing occurred. She walked over to the side of the bed and pulled back the covers.

"You're about to go to bed? We haven't eaten dinner yet!"

"I know but I need to lay down for a while. Dinner is all ready for you guys and I'll be down soon," Keisha crawled in bed and nestled herself in between her six hundred count Egyptian sheets.

"Alright babe," David replied, walking out of their bedroom and back down the steps. She waited until she heard him in the kitchen before she flipped the covers back and got out of bed.

# pretty skeletons

She began to experience an excruciating headache and needed the constant pounding in her head to stop. She walked into the master bathroom. The coolness of the marble floor tickled her manicured feet as she opened the medicine cabinet in search of something to calm the pounding in her head. Keisha reached for the bottle of Ibuprofen but could tell it was empty when she picked it up. She threw the used pill bottle in the trash and then searched the cabinet for something else. She came across a bottle of sleeping pills prescribed to her husband. Since there was nothing else in the medicine cabinet, that had to be sufficient enough to soothe her headache. She decided to pop a few in her mouth. She planned on being asleep in a hurry anyway. That way, she wouldn't have to think about anything.

# chapter 9

“ “ Are you ready to start the session today?” Dr. Karen asked.

Keisha started shaking, inhaled deeply, and then forced all of the air out of her lungs. She thumbed through the pages of her diary until she came to the entry where she'd left off. She glanced up from the page and saw Dr. Karen give her an approving nod. So she looked down, took another deep breath, and started reading.

He did it again. He touched me like he did two weeks ago but this time it was different. Instead of him playing it off like his touching me was an accident, he touched me in a different way. This time he meant to do it. The way he touched my behind and the space in between my legs made me feel very weird. For some reason, by the look in his eyes, I knew his touch this time was on purpose. There wasn't any mistake in that at all. I had this feeling deep in my stomach that there was more to it than he admitted and I was fearful of what he was gonna do next. I'm so scared and terrified and I really don't know what to do. All I know is we're going down a path that is not good at all.

Keisha attempted to continue reading from her diary but became choked up with emotion. Her persistent sighs turned into intermittent hyperventilation as she struggled to gain composure. Going back down memory lane proved to be difficult and uncertain. Revealing her past was painful and she wasn't sure if she was strong enough to pull those calloused scabs off of the old wounds of her life.

“Keisha, listen to me. I want you to close your eyes and breathe. Just breathe,” Karen reminded her. “We don't have to talk about anything that you don't want to. Okay? Remember that!”

Keisha closed her eyes and did as she instructed. She had come to respect Dr. Karen's judgment as a therapist. She tried to relax and gain calmness so she could proceed, but she still found herself unable to open up her mouth to discuss exactly how she felt. "I don't know if I can go back and work through this. I'm not strong enough," she sighed.

"That's understandable because going back to the past hurts especially when we've experienced a great deal of trauma but, when we make the decision not to go back and work through our skeletons, our lives never really get any better. They tend to get worse."

Keisha shook her head in disagreement with her statement.

"I still don't know if I can do this."

"I know this is hard but believe me I know firsthand about the necessity of dealing with situations in the past."

"What do you mean?"

"When I was a little girl, my father's best friend and our neighbor used to touch me inappropriately. When I got older and started developing into a woman, he seized the opportunity to take the one thing from me I considered sacred and I hated him! I hated the fact that I never had enough courage to speak up about what took place, practically in my parent's backyard. So, I know where you're coming from," Dr. Karen explained as she paused a moment to look sincerely in Keisha's face.

Her admission took Keisha totally by surprise. She never expected her therapist to have gone through a similar situation. "Wow, I would've never known..."

"Trust me, Keisha. I know you signed up and decided to come to me in the beginning because you want help to deal with all of this and you have to understand how committed I am to doing just that. Some may call my methods of treatment unconventional, but I don't care because I treat everyone with the same techniques that helped me."

Keisha sat there and covered her face with her delicate hands as Dr. Karen spoke.

"I can empathize with you. You're probably going through a sea of emotions right now and there's a part of you saying you're better off leaving the past alone but, then, there's another part of you pleading to deal with the hidden things in your life that has secretly tormented you for years. Revisiting your past is necessary in your course of treatment. It will get better," Karen nodded.

Keisha understood Karen was not only a professional but also had the background to deal with people like her, but she still wasn't confident she could be helped. She wanted to hold on to the notion that things would get better but she had a feeling they were getting ready to be a lot worse.

"I understand everything that you're telling me but I just can't open up anymore. I have to leave Karen." Keisha said as she stood up abruptly and gathered her things. Karen glanced at her watch and wondered why she was leaving so soon.

"Keisha your session isn't over for another twenty-five minutes, why are you leaving?"

"Because I have to. I hope you understand. Goodbye." Keisha replied and walked out of Dr. Karen's office. She usually always stopped by the secretary's office to talk or schedule another appointment but she didn't stop until she reached her car in the parking lot.

Keisha broke down as soon as she closed her car door. She never imagined that re-reading her own words would hurt so much. Most of the things she'd endured occurred over fifteen years ago but, while in Dr. Karen's office, it felt as though they happened last night. These feelings and emotions were the very things frightening her. They were supposed to be buried and never to be revisited again. From time to time, she would think about everything but she did her best to push those memories far out of her mind. She worked so hard to reinvent herself by the time she graduated college and met her husband David, she had done away with the old Keisha. She'd managed to suppress the binge drinking, pill-popping, drug addicted Keisha and replaced her with a brand new person.

She stuck her key in the ignition then tried to start her car and drive away but her mind raced and she found herself unable to move. Her tears of sadness and hurt turned to anger in an instant. She thought about everything she'd gone through and how one man caused all the pain she felt in her heart. The one man who was supposed to take care of her was the same one who took advantage of her, all the while calling the name of

# JESSICA A. ROBINSON

Jesus. That's why she didn't care about Jessie and she sure didn't care about the God he claimed to serve.

Keisha glanced down at her silver and diamond Bulova watch and realized she was already late to pick up her children from school. She pulled out her cell phone and dialed Kennedi's number. She was happy her sister answered on the first ring.

"What's up Keesh?" Kennedi asked.

"Hey sis, I was wondering if you were at home?"

"Yeah, I'm home. What's up?"

"Can you do me a favor and pick up the kids? I'm running late coming from work."

"Yeah, that's no problem. Do you need me to keep them for a while until you get home and get situated?"

"Thanks Kennedi! That would be great."

Keisha hung up the phone, relieved she wouldn't have to rush across town. Besides, she didn't want to have to hear their little mouths complaining about her tardiness anyway. That was the advantage of having her baby sister living so close to their school and she appreciated Kennedi because it gave her an opportunity to do the things she needed to do and get settled before they came home.

She pulled into the parking lot of Starbucks and decided to stop for a white chocolate mocha. No matter how she felt at the moment, she figured she always had time for a little coffee. She was glad the parking lot only contained a few cars which meant less crowding in the shop. She really didn't feel like running into anyone either.

Keisha walked up to the counter and ordered her favorite drink. She then found a comfortable spot in the far corner and sat down. She seemed to have made it just in time because, as soon as she took her jacket off, a rush of people came in. Keisha watched as the line, that was clear out of the store, dwindled down to a few customers. Those remaining seemed to be business men, probably stopping in to purchase something to rejuvenate them during their busy event-filled day. Somehow, she focused in on the last one in line who stood there waiting patiently for his order. She studied the light skinned man dressed in a three piece suit, convinced she knew him from somewhere. For a second, she didn't have a clue then it finally hit her. She got up from the table and walked over to him.

"Eric?" Keisha tapped his shoulder from behind. He turned around and began to smile from ear to ear revealing his dimples he'd had since birth.

"Oh my gosh. Keisha, is that really you?" Eric asked as he extended his arms and gave her a big hug.

"It's me, in the flesh. What are you doing here?" Keisha asked.

"Well, I'm here in town on business. I'm an executive banker with PNC and they've brought me here to train the branches in the city on the new procedures and systems. I assume that you live here now?"

"Yes, I live here in the city with my husband and two children. I really can't believe it's you! I honestly thought I would never see you again!" Keisha blinked her eyes several times to make sure she wasn't imagining things. Her best friend actually stood right in front of her face. She hadn't seen or talked to him since the day she left for her Aunt Darlene's house.

"I know. I can't believe it either. I honestly never thought I'd see you again."

"...and we run into each at the same Starbuck's. Wow!"

"How about that?"

Keisha smirked while Eric ordered his coffee and a plain piece of cheesecake then joined her at the table.

"Well, let me be the first to say, you look exactly the same. You still got a big head!" Eric announced and caused Keisha to laugh.

"I see you still crackin' jokes!" She smiled.

"I wouldn't be me if I didn't!" Keisha took a sip of her coffee then placed the container back down on the table. She glanced over at Eric who started to eat his dessert. As she watched him consume a few pieces, she almost felt as though she was in a dream. Eric was the one person she never thought she would see again yet so desired to find him. From the moment they moved from their apartment in Youngstown to Columbus, she always thought about him and Ms. Gina. Her mind often wondered to how they were doing and what they were up to. Keisha then thought about who Eric hung out with since she's moved.

"I can see you're still greedy," Keisha laughed as Eric was almost done with his cheesecake when she made that statement.

"If my memory serves me correctly, you were the greedy one. Eating everything in sight," he replied.

"I couldn't help it. Your momma's food was so good."

"So catch me up on the present," Eric said as he finished the last bite and pushed his plate to the side.

"I graduated college with a business degree. I'm married, have twins, and I work for one of the biggest law firms in the city. That's me in a nutshell."

"Wow! You've done a lot. That's great!"

"How about you?" Keisha asked.

"I graduated from Howard, went back to college, got my Master's in Accounting, and I am now employed by PNC Bank in Pittsburgh," Eric explained.

"That sounds like an important responsibility."

"It is. Since the banks are converting from one system to another, it's my job to bring them up to speed with the way I do things. How long have you been in Akron?"

"I've been here since college. I moved here once I left Columbus."

"So here we are, both in the same city at the same time, and had no clue at all. I thought you were still in Columbus."

"Nope. Not at all."

"I did look for you online in the yellow pages but it still had your aunt and uncle's address as your last known."

"I've been unlisted for quite some time," Keisha answered. She wasn't the least surprised her address didn't show up in search engines online. In fact, she did everything she had to do to make sure it did not.

"That explains why you were so hard to reach."

"So you've told me about everything else but are you married with kids?"

Eric shook his head to indicate no.

"Are you serious?"

"Yeah, I guess the good Lord doesn't want me to get married yet. It's okay! I know my singleness is just a season and He'll send me my wife soon."

"Still in church?"

"You know it. I actually attend this really nice church called Mt. Arat in Pittsburgh. It's about fifteen minutes from my condo."

"Wow," Keisha replied.

"Do you and your family attend church anywhere?"

"My husband and children go to New Word Christian Center. So how's Ms. Gina?" Keisha asked and took a big sip of her coffee that was almost ice cold. She began to tap her leg feverishly as she started to tell her about his mom.

"My mom is doing great. She's still in Youngstown for the moment but she's actually in the process of relocating to be closer to me. I just had a meeting with a real estate agent that's next door to where I live."

"That's really great. I'm so glad to hear that. I forgot to tell you Kennedi and Alonzo are both here too."

"Sweet! We definitely need to all get together sometime but, before I go, let's exchange numbers so we can keep in touch." Eric pulled out his Palm Treo and punched the numbers Keisha gave him in his phone. She did the same and they both got up from the table and hugged each other.

"It was so good seeing you Keisha," he smiled.

"You too!"

"Take care!" Eric said and walked out of the door.

After the tumultuous day she just had, running into her old best friend was the temporary relief she needed. She was happy to see he did well for himself. She was also glad to know Ms. Gina was still around too. Just thinking about Eric and Ms. Gina made her think about the past and life before her mom's overdose. During those times, she could truly say she experienced happiness. Even though they lived in a crowded two bedroom apartment in the projects and her mother was a drug addict, life was still better than being at Jessie's big pretty house.

# chapter 10

Keisha took the short drive home from Starbucks and saw David's truck already sitting in the driveway. She glanced down at her watch and realized he must've had an early day. He usually worked late hours during the week. When she walked through the door, she was relieved to see her husband had ordered a pizza. She definitely didn't feel like cooking anything.

"You must've read my mind, baby." Keisha walked up to David and kissed him.

"I had an early day at the shop so, when I came home and saw you and the kids weren't here, I decided to cook us some pizza." David laughed as he pretended to take a bow for his efforts.

"Thank you. Everything smells great!" She smiled.

"Where's Katrina and D.J.?" David asked as he pulled a stack of paper plates out of a plastic bag and set them on the dinner table. Just as Keisha got ready to answer him, the doorbell rang. "That's probably Kennedi now. I had her pick them up because I was running late."

Keisha opened the door and was bombarded with hugs and kisses from her own children and nephew Quincy.

"I missed you too!" Keisha said as she bent down to embrace all three of them.

"Mommy, we're hungry," D.J. announced.

"Well, go get washed up because your dad ordered pizza." The kids screamed in unison.

"Kennedi, we have more than enough food. You and Quincy can stay if you want."

Kennedi rubbed her hands together and smiled. "You don't have to tell me twice! You know I'm not gonna pass up any pizza."

The kids raced each other up the stairs and Kennedi turned to face her sister before she walked in the kitchen.

"So, what was that the other day?" she asked as she lowered her voice.

"What are you talking about?" Keisha responded, looking at her sister like she was confused by the inquiry.

Kennedi looked behind her to make sure David wasn't in hearing distance and whispered, "Applebee's." Keisha smacked her lips and waved her sister away.

"That was nothing. Just two old friends catching up. That's it. And I already told you that anyway."

"Okay, I can see you're irritated so I'm gonna leave it alone but I was surprised to see you sitting at the table chatting with someone who you couldn't stand to be around."

"I know how I used to be but people can change."

"Yeah, I guess. Oh, before I forget, do you have any plans this weekend?"

"No. Not that I know of."

"Okay cool."

"Why do you want to go somewhere?" Keisha asked.

"No I was just wondering if you had any plans that's all." Kennedi replied. Keisha looked at her with a confused look on her face.

"Alright, well my schedule is completely free so if you should feel the need to want to go somewhere, then let me know. I'll get my mother-in-law to watch the kids."

"Cool sis."

David called everyone to join him and they walked into the kitchen acting as if their mini conversation never happened. Keisha felt relieved her nosey sister didn't take it upon herself to press the issue because Malik was someone from her past that David didn't know about. If she chose to bring up Malik, she would in turn tell him about the drugs as well as everything else associated with life in Columbus and she didn't choose to reveal to that to him. In her mind, it didn't even exist in her timeline.

## pretty skeletons

Keisha helped David fix everyone's plate then they all sat down together and ate. The twins went on and on about their day at school until David sprang forward in his chair with something to say.

"Oh yeah, babe, I forgot to tell you. Alonzo came in the shop today. He had me cut his hair and line up his beard."

"Oh, that's cool. He looked so crazy with his hair getting long. I've been meaning to go over to see him."

"He said he's doing good. He's been back to work and everything but took off this weekend." David wiped his mouth with a napkin. Keisha looked up from her food and questioned David.

"Why would he take off if he just started back?" Keisha looked over her sister, who shook her head at David. He obviously didn't understand her signal because he continued on with what he said with a confused look on his face.

"He took off so y'all can drive home this weekend." David finished while glancing back at Kennedi, who looked worried.

"Excuse me?" Keisha asked, obviously not knowing what David meant.

"Kennedi, what is David talking about?" Keisha turned her attention toward her sister who cut her eyes at David then smiled.

"Umm… Well, that's what I was getting ready to tell you. Zoe and I talked and figured, this weekend, we should go home to visit with Darlene and Jessie."

Keisha's nostrils flared as she sat across from her sister. David sent all the children to go upstairs and play hoping they wouldn't hear or be concerned with what the adults were talking about.

"So, how long y'all been planning this without telling me?" Keisha asked as she leaned across the table.

"Keisha, we haven't known we were going for long. But, Uncle Jessie called us and we really need to go and see him."

"You already know I don't wanna see that man. And, on top of it all, you went behind my back to plan this trip when you know I don't wanna go in the first place!"

"If we would've told you, would you still wanna go with us?" Kennedi asked. Keisha crossed her arms and didn't respond at all. "My point exactly. Look, it's only for one weekend. It's not gonna kill you to go home. I think it will be good that we go. This way, all of us can talk and work everything out," Kennedi explained yet Keisha pushed her chair back from the table and stood up.

"Whatever Kennedi! I'm not working nothing out!" Keisha replied and walked out of the kitchen. She jogged upstairs and retreated to her bedroom. She shut the door behind her and began to pace. She was steaming hot and furious that her sister and brother planned something behind her back without her input. To make matters worse her husband even knew what they were up to. The more she thought about the situation, the more she figured Jessie had to be the one behind all the shady moves to get her to come home.

Keisha walked over to their bed and sat down on the edge in attempt to calm her nerves and growing irritation but that didn't seem to do anything except make her feel worse. Her heart raced and her breathing increased in rate with an irregular rhythm. She tried to close her eyes and relax herself but, every time her eyelids shut, she couldn't help but think about the impending trip she didn't want to make.

Keisha went into the bathroom and opened up the medicine cabinet in search of David's sleeping pills but discovered an empty bottle. She couldn't believe they were already gone and remembered only taking a few to help her fall asleep from time to time. She shuffled various bottles around until she stumbled upon a brand new bottle of Vicodin prescribed to David when he injured his back while working in factory a few years before opening the shop.

She remembered when he first came home from the doctor with his prescription. She worried about having easy access to such pain killers, thinking it would be too much temptation for her. Before she'd done her stint in rehab, those were the very pills that made up her usual "cocktail." She used to be afraid of being so close to her weakness, thinking it would cause her to relapse. But, over the years, she's done surprisingly well and never had the urge to take any.

She pulled the bottle from its place in the cabinet and popped the top off. For a moment, she contemplated putting the bottle back and going back downstairs to join her sister and husband. But, before she could think, she tipped the bottle over and dropped four of the white oblong tablets in her hand and then returned the bottle to its place.

Keisha filled her glass halfway with water and swallowed each individually. She allowed the faucet to run and splashed water on her face. When she dried off and opened her eyes, she realized what she had done – took four while Vicodin were one of the drugs she vowed she to never touch again. She had just submitted to her biggest tempter – prescription pills despite knowing they were given to her husband for the back aches he experienced from time to time and were only given to someone if they were in pain. Even though she wasn't in any apparent physical hurt, she considered herself to be in much more emotional pain and felt she well within her right to take something that would help take the edge off. Besides, she didn't consider four pills to be a relapse, especially when she used to take a drug cocktail just to get high.

Keisha slipped on her pajamas and didn't even bother to go back downstairs. She got into her bed and let the pills take her to a relaxed state of mind. She had a feeling deep down in the pit of her stomach that she was in for the worst weekend ever. The next day, Kennedi and Alonzo picked Keisha up bright and early from her house. She didn't say much to them and she hoped they would take the hint and let her at least enjoy the trip in complete silence since it wouldn't be quiet at their aunt's house once they arrived.

Keisha could hear Kennedi calling her name for the last three minutes but she didn't bother to acknowledge her. She kept her eyes closed and increased the volume on her iPod, hoping her annoying sister would get the hint and leave her alone. Of course she didn't and kept saying her name, which only increased Keisha irritation. She figured the only way she could put an end to her sister's nagging was to respond.

"What Kennedi? What do you want?" Keisha asked.

"You didn't hear me callin' you all this time?"

Keisha removed her headphones out of her ear and replied, "No, I just heard you."

The flat smile Keisha flashed let her sister know she heard her the entire time but didn't manage to say a word. Her sister's blatant ignorance caused her to roll her eyes.

"We're almost to Aunt Darlene's house and you haven't said a word. Are you gonna say anything?"

"No, I don't feel like talking," Keisha answered.

"So, you're just not gonna say anything the entire time we're here?" Alonzo asked as he took an exit on the I-71 to lead them directly to their aunt's house.

"Look, I'm in this truck with y'all? Ain't I? You better be glad I'm even here after what y'all pulled." Keisha shut off her iPod and stuffed it in her pink Juicy Couture purse. She had a feeling she wasn't going to get a chance to listen to it any time soon.

"Come on, Keisha. You know we had to do it like this. Otherwise, you would've made up some excuse not to come," Alonzo said as Kennedi nodded her head. She couldn't stand it when her brother and sister joined forces against her.

"Whatever, Zoe. You two planning to come home behind my back was just wrong and you know it!" She crossed her arms.

"With the way you act about visiting, you really gave us no choice," Kennedi reiterated.

Keisha didn't respond. She turned her head to look out the window and was truly at a loss for words. She knew they only wanted to come home because of Jessie's illness but, as far as she was concerned, she didn't see it that way. Seeing Darlene and Jessie evoked a pain Keisha felt in the pit of her stomach.

They rode in silence until Alonzo made a right-hand turn onto their street.

"Now, I know you and Uncle Jessie don't get along but can you at least try while we're here," he pleaded.

Keisha took the opportunity to roll her eyes and huff. "Fine! Whatever you want!"

"Thank you!" Alonzo responded.

Keisha agreed to try her best to get along with him but, if he did or said anything to provoke her nerves, there was no telling how she'd respond. Keisha decided to uphold the promise she'd made Alonzo but wasn't sure how long she would be able to do so.

He pulled in the driveway and parked next to Jessie's cherry wine Cadillac STS. Keisha exhaled and got out of the car. She looked toward the front of the house and saw Jessie standing in the doorway. She had a feeling she was in for a long weekend.

Once they all made their way up to the porch with their bags, Jessie opened the glass screen door and smiled.

"I'm so glad you all could make it," Jessie said as Keisha smacked her lips. Her sister looked over and cut her eyes.

"We're happy we could come, Uncle Jessie! Where's Auntie?" Kennedi asked.

"She's in the kitchen finishing dinner."

Kennedi walked past Jessie to go inside of the house while Alonzo stopped in the doorway to give him a big hug. Keisha tried to squeeze past him and go straight inside the house but they blocked the entrance. She stood there with her arms crossed as the two men embraced.

"I'm so glad you could come here and see me," Jessie said.

"And I'm just glad you're alright."

"I wouldn't miss coming to see you for the world Unc," Alonzo replied and Keisha rolled her eyes. She honestly hoped they would be done with their soap opera reunion soon so she could get in the house. After they finished, Keisha picked up her overnight bag and attempted to enter but Jessie stood in the door once again blocking her.

"Hello Keisha, it has been a very long time since I've saw you," Jessie said.

"Yup. It sure has," she answered, wishing he would just move out of the way.

If you ask me, it hasn't been long enough. Honestly, I think I could go a lifetime without seeing that fool. And even that, still wouldn't be long enough. His very presence makes me want to throw up.

"I see you're trying to get in the house and you don't wanna talk to me but it's good to have you home." He stated and moved to the side so she could walk through. Before she could get too far, he whispered, "You look even better than you did back then."

Keisha wished she hadn't heard the ignorant comment but she decided to act like she didn't. She couldn't believe he was already starting with her and she hadn't even been in the house five good minutes. She could only imagine what else he would manage to say by the end of this visit.

Later that day, Keisha took a deep breath as she took a seat at the dinner table. Aunt Darlene had prepared a feast and wasn't going to let anyone eat until they all sat down together. Family dinner was the ritual Darlene adhered to and it had always been that way. Keisha never saw what the big deal was about but knew her aunt wouldn't have it any other way. Keisha didn't mind sitting down to eat dinner with her husband and two children, but with the two people she couldn't stand was a completely different story.

"Aunt Darlene, you cooked a huge meal. Are you sure we're the only ones coming to dinner?" Alonzo asked as he stared at the expansive spread across the table. She prepared fried chicken, ham, green beans, macaroni and cheese, black-eyed peas, and hot water cornbread.

"I know it's a lot of food but I couldn't help myself. I got excited when I started thinking about all of you coming home," Darlene smiled.

"Smelling all this food is making me hungry," Jessie laughed as he pretended to rub his stomach.

"Alonzo, can you bless it for us?" Darlene asked as she motioned for everyone to join hands. Alonzo bowed his head and began to pray.

"Lord, we come asking a special blessing over the food we're about to receive. Bless the hands that prepared it. In Jesus name. Amen."

"Amen. Maybe y'all need to come home every week so your aunt can cook like this more often," Jessie said as he cut his eyes at Darlene and she smacked her lips. "You see I'm losing weight!"

"Yeah, Uncle Jessie! You are a little thinner than usual," Kennedi commented.

# pretty skeletons

"I know. Ever since my kidneys have been deteriorating, I haven't been able to keep my size up," he explained.

"It doesn't matter. You still look good!" Alonzo replied. Jessie pressed his lips together and offered him a smile.

"Thanks, I really appreciate that!"

Keisha didn't bother to take part in their conversation. She figured she did her part by not getting into an argument with Jessie. She'd made a promise to Alonzo about not being disrespectful while they were there and felt like the only way to keep it was by speaking as least as possible. She knew she would eventually have something to say something at some point but, until then, she planned on keeping her mouth closed.

"So Keisha, it's good to have you home. I haven't seen you in years," Jessie said as she suddenly became engrossed in her plate.

"Oh, I'm sorry! Did you say something?" Keisha asked as if she just tuned in to their conversation. Jessie knew Keisha had heard every word he said but it still didn't matter. He put down his fork and repeated his statement.

"I said, it's good to have you home. It's been a very long time since I've laid eyes on you," Jessie replied and winked at her. She looked around to see if her brother, sister, or even aunt caught his slick gesture but they all seemed to be caught up enjoying their food.

Keisha ignored him and started to eat when Aunt Darlene spoke out.

"Your sister told me the twins are in Kindergarten already. I bet they've gotten so big," she replied and dabbed her mouth with a linen napkin.

"Yeah, they're real big now. I used to be able to hold them both in my arms. Now, I tell them to forget about it," Keisha responded. She was glad her aunt interjected because she could feel her previous conversation going in a bad direction.

"Do you have any pictures? I would love to see them," Darlene asked. Keisha searched through a few of her pockets until she came to her change wallet which contained a small photograph. She handed the photo over to her, which immediately brought a smile to her face.

"Wow. They are absolutely beautiful. I think they are good mix of you and David," Darlene commented.

"That's what I always tell her," Kennedi said as she shot her sister a look.

"Yeah, I'll admit when they were little, they looked exactly like me. Now, they don't at all," Keisha smiled. If she wasn't happy about anything else taking place that weekend, at least, she could be glad about her children. The smile she temporarily wore turned upside down when she watched her Uncle Jessie reach for the picture then stare at it. He studied it intently and spoke.

"I beg to differ."

"Excuse me?" Keisha asked as her nostrils started to flare.

"What I meant to say is your kids are precious. That Katrina, she sure looks just like you did when you were her age. She is beautiful!" Jessie continued as he looked at Keisha and emphasized every word. She could feel her blood begin to boil with each passing moment and could see he wasn't ashamed of his sly comments at all. She noticed how he stared at her with that "look" in eyes. The same look he had when he crept into her bedroom at night, the exact same glare he possessed when he touched her inappropriately, and the same lustful look that haunted her every time she dreamt about him. Keisha pushed her chair away from the table and sprang up.

"Look, I can't do this. I gotta go before I say something I'll regret," Keisha explained. She felt it was better for her to excuse herself away from the dinner table rather than stay and run the risk of offending the wrong person.

"Keisha, why are you leaving? You haven't even touched your food yet!" Darlene expressed with a confused look on her face. Keisha couldn't believe her aunt always chose to play the clueless role. That was one of the reasons she irritated her most of the time.

"I know, but I need to remove myself before it's too late so I think that's my cue to go up to my room," Keisha said while she walked away leaving both her brother and sister's mouths wide open. Even Darlene had an astonished look like she didn't have any idea what set her off. As Keisha slammed her door and sat down on her old bed, her mind took her to the time when she spoke up and told her aunt the truth.

She hadn't planned on saying anything but, when she popped up pregnant a month before her sixteenth birthday, she felt she had no choice. Keisha remembered her period hadn't come for three entire months. She bought a pregnancy test only to confirm what she already knew in her heart. She was in the tenth grade, almost sixteen, and pregnant with her "uncle's" baby. She didn't tell anybody anything for a couple of weeks, secretly hoping the baby would somehow abort itself. But, when it didn't, she pulled the only person she could pull to the side – Jessie.

Of course, he freaked out and didn't know what to do until, one day, he finally came up with the "perfect plan." He suggested telling Darlene that Keisha was in fact pregnant but by Malik since Keisha had been caught messing around with him. He prepared some long drawn out speech about how she needed to abort the baby because she was young and still had her life to live, figuring that would be the end of it. Keisha agreed to the situation because Jessie threatened to do something bad to her brother and sister if she didn't. Even though she agreed to go along with his treacherous scheme, she felt like maybe it was the prime opportunity to expose her uncle for the low down, dirty man he was. She felt maybe it was time to finally muster up enough courage to be honest about the molestation that had taken place under their roof. Besides, she considered Jessie's plan to convince his wife that she was pregnant by Malik was faulty anyway when she wasn't even allowed out of their sight without some form of a chaperone. They only had an opportunity to have sex a few times and, even then, it was an absolute miracle they had been allowed to see each other. Since her aunt's rules were so strict to begin with she knew her auntie would definitely see the loophole and Jessie's lie would unravel right before his eyes. But, when she approached her, she received a very different response.

"So you've been messing around with Malik, even after we said you weren't allowed to see him. And, now you're pregnant, huh?" Darlene asked as she sat in her black leather recliner chair. Keisha remembered how sweat beads ran down

# JESSICA A. ROBINSON

her forehead while she stood before her aunt who prided herself in being a strict disciplinarian. She remained silent with a mean glare on her face as Darlene stared at her from head to toe.

"Did you hear me talking to you? I said you have let this little stupid thug knock you up?"

Still, she didn't say anything in response to her aunt's accusation. She continued to stare at her while occasionally rolling her eyes at the enemy.

"Keisha, don't make me repeat myself. I said…"

"Aunt Darlene, Malik didn't get me pregnant," Keisha said as a single tear rolled down her face. Her uncle began to look over at her with a confused countenance as he waited to her what she would say.

"Well, if he didn't get your pregnant then who did?" Darlene asked. Keisha closed her eyes and took a few deep breaths. She knew what she getting ready to confess was about to disturb her life even more but she didn't care. She already felt she was living in hell residing under their roof anyway. To her, it couldn't get much worse.

Keisha opened her eyes and finally built up enough courage to admit the truth.

"Uncle Jessie," Keisha replied.

"What?" Darlene asked in some sort of denial.

"You asked me, who I was pregnant by, and I answered you! I said Uncle Jessie!" Keisha stated matter of factly. Jessie threw his hands up in the air as if he were appalled at the newly discovered revelation.

"I can't believe this!" he shouted as he crossed his arms over his broad chest. Darlene rose from her recliner chair.

"That has got to be the most ridiculous thing I've ever heard. Are you trying to stand here and tell me that you're not only pregnant but it's by my husband?" Darlene asked. Keisha quickly glanced over at Jessie who looked like he wanted to strangle her on the spot.

"Yes!" Keisha answered and couldn't stop the tears from falling. Darlene turned to face Jessie and asked, "what is she talking about?"

"I don't know, Darlene. I never touched this girl and I would never even think of doing something like that to her. Believe

me! The bottom line is Keisha has gone out there out here and created this problem with Malik and now we have to fix it."
Keisha heard Jessie's lie and lost it all in that moment.

"I wasn't even going to say anything but I caught Malik and Keisha fooling around before when I came home from work early. And, I wasn't going to say anything about it because I had already given them a talk but, now, I feel like it needs to be said."

"Oh my God! Why are you lying Jessie? You know I didn't get pregnant by no boy! Tell the truth!" Keisha stared at Jessie hoping he would finally admit the things he'd been doing to her since she'd moved into the house. She looked into his eyes, hoping he had an ounce of dignity left but he stared right back at her and continued to lie. Then to add insult to injury, her aunt believed him and went along with his plan to abort the baby.
Loud pounding on the door interrupted her thoughts and brought her back to the present.

"Keisha! It's me, open up!" Alonzo said from the other side. She sat silent for a second without answering him right away.

"Bro, I'm cool. I just need to relax," she finally replied. She thought her answer would be sufficient but he continued to knock.

"Come on and open up this door," he asked.

"You better be alone." Keisha got up and turned the lock to let him in.

"It's cool. I'm by myself." He held up his hands and walked into the room shutting the squeaky wooden door behind him.

"What was all that about downstairs?"

"I really don't want to talk about it, Zoe!"

"I can't believe you and Uncle Jessie don't get along after all these years. I thought you would have a better relationship by now, seeing we're adults."

"Honestly, I don't think we'll ever get along. I can't stand to be in the same room with him." Keisha crossed her arms and leaned further back on the bed.

"Well, after what I saw, I can believe that. You gonna at least come down and finish dinner?"

"Naw, I think I'll call it a night." Keisha pretended to yawn as they both stood at the same time.

"Are you sure you cool?"

Keisha shook her head and unzipped her overnight bag located next to the bed.

"Alonzo, I'm fine," Keisha reassured her brother. He left her and went back downstairs. Even though she had reiterated she was fine, that couldn't be further from how she really felt. The truth, she was miserable and more stressed than ever before. Keisha pulled out her pajama set and went to place it on the bed when David's bottle of Vicodin pills fell out of the bag. She'd almost forgotten she packed them but was glad she did. Keisha figured a hand full would definitely help her get some rest.

# chapter 11

Keisha opened her eyes and realized she'd slept the entire night without waking up at all. She was glad for the uninterrupted sleep but not happy about the excruciating headaches she experienced. For a few minutes, she laid still hoping it would stop but the throbbing continued.

She decided to get up and go downstairs since her headache wasn't trying to go away. When she walked into the kitchen, everyone was already at the table dressed and eating breakfast.

"The dead has arisen," Alonzo laughed.

"Shut up!" Keisha simply replied.

"We tried to wake you up almost an hour and a half ago but you were knocked out," Kennedi explained. Keisha took her seat at the table next to her sister and poured herself a glass of orange juice.

"I see everyone's dressed. Where are you going this early?" Keisha asked as Aunt Darlene brought her a plate of eggs, sausage, and two pieces of wheat toast.

"We're going to go over to Pastor Jones' and visit with him and his family. He's excited to see you all," Jessie said but Keisha quickly rolled her eyes.

"I'm not going to Pastor Jones' house with y'all," Keisha proclaimed.

"Why not? You have more than enough time to go upstairs and get yourself ready," Darlene explained as she cleared dirty plates from the table.

"I have a headache and I'm not going. I think I still need to lie down for a while," Keisha replied.

"Okay Keisha. I know pastor will be disappointed he won't get to see you but he'll understand you're not feeling well."

She finished her breakfast in silence as Darlene went on and on about how wonderful Pastor Jones is and all the great things he's done for the church. Jessie even chimed in with a few praises about his beloved pastor like the man was God himself and she realized that even though years had passed things were still the same. They still worshipped the ground he walked on even though he wasn't anywhere near perfect, Keisha thought as she began to recall her last encounter with him.

After the pregnancy, abortion, and years of sexual abuse she endured, Keisha decided to tell her pastor. Especially after attempting to tell her aunt proved to be unsuccessful.
She scheduled a meeting with him and told him everything. Keisha didn't leave one single detail out. She remembered how he stared at her intensely for about five minutes, with his hand folded, before he said anything.

"I can't believe what you just told me about your uncle, Keisha."

"I know it sounds a little hard to believe but I promise you I'm telling you the truth!" Keisha pleaded as she looked him square in his eyes. She needed him to look beyond everything and to see she told the truth. She didn't know him as well as her aunt and uncle did but she observed him to be a pretty fair man who definitely prided himself in doing the right thing. She hoped this time would be no different. But what came out of his mouth was totally different then what she expected to hear.

"I'm having an extremely hard time believing what you've just said and an even more difficult time with the fact that you said you've suffered all this at the hands of Deacon Jessie."

"I understand it sounds crazy but that's why I came to you because I knew you would listen to me," Keisha said, desperately trying to get her point across. Pastor Jones took a moment to collect his thoughts then leaned back in his big leather chair.

"Well I've listened to everything you've said, and I honestly have to say I don't think you're telling me the truth," he replied, causing Keisha's mouth and heart to sink the floor.

"What?" Keisha asked.

"I mean, Deacon Jessie is one of the most celebrated and dedicated clergy men in this church and I just don't see how he would be capable of doing something like that to you," Pastor Jones replied as his face turned from pure concern to anger in the matter of seconds. Keisha leaned up in her chair and tears started to run down her face.

"I promise you. I'm telling the truth. You have to believe me!"

"Okay Keisha, now even if everything you were saying was the truth, do you know what that type of information could do if it got into the wrong hands?"

"What do you mean?" Keisha asked.

"This could destroy you. It could destroy your uncle. But, most of all it could potentially destroy this church. So we need to make sure this conversation doesn't get out to anyone else."

"So what are you trying to say pastor?"

"It's simple. We're going to grab hands and pray. After I say, Amen, we're going to act as if this none of this ever happened."

And, that's exactly what Pastor Jones did. He managed to act as if their conversation had evaporated into thin air. From that moment on, Keisha kept her mouth shut about the entire situation because no one seemed to believe her anyway.

"Keisha, we're about to leave. If you need anything, just give us a call. We'll be back later on," Darlene said as she reached over the table, grabbed her keys and then walked out the door while Keisha snapped back into reality.

"Okay, see ya later!" Keisha said as she watched everyone walk out the front door and get into Jessie's black cherry Cadillac and drive away. She was glad that they were all gone. She could have some real peace and quiet. She didn't have to be interrogated by Darlene and she didn't have to hear any slick remarks from Jessie.

Every time she thought about how he managed to push all the right buttons to irritate her at dinner made her mad all over again. She was glad he left, even if only for a couple hours. Keisha took advantage of the time alone and took a nap. When she woke up, she realized everyone was still gone, so she went downstairs to the living room and decided watch television.

While flipping through channels, she noticed the old wooden bookcase that contained their family photo albums sitting next to the entertainment center. Aunt Darlene used to keep it in the den with her other actual bookcases.

She went over and picked up a few of the albums and brought them to where she sat on the couch. Keisha opened up the black one that appeared too brand new and started looking through pages of pictures she'd never seen. It included pictures of Alonzo, when he was a baby. Some of Rita and Darlene sprinkled the pages as well. She found herself confused as she stared at the photos because she didn't remember her aunt being around at all. She thought that she'd met her aunt for the first time when she initially taken custody of them but seeing these images made her realize that what her aunt used to tell her was the truth. She smiled as she looked at the pictures of her mother and Darlene together then wondered why her mother never talked about her sister. When she asked Rita if she had any siblings she told Keisha that she was the only child. She also began to wonder why she and Kennedi were never in any of those photos.

"Bring back memories, don't they?" Jessie said.

Keisha looked up to see him standing in the doorway of the living room. She had been so consumed she didn't hear anyone come in.

"What are you doing here? You're supposed to be gone." Keisha snapped the book shut and rolled her eyes. Jessie leaned against the doorway and smiled.

"I had your aunt drop me off before they went out to lunch with Pastor Jones. I'm not feeling too well," he replied as he rubbed his stomach and then laughed. Keisha didn't find anything he said too amusing so her facial expression remained emotionless and tight.

"You don't look sick to me," Keisha huffed.

"Well, just because I don't appear to be sick to you doesn't mean that I'm not," Jessie said as he continued to grin, only adding to her irritation.

"Whatever. Why did you really come home early? Because I was here, huh?" Keisha asked and shook her head.

"I came home for two reasons. One being I really need to rest because I've been running around too much. Second, I think we need to talk."

# pretty skeletons

"As far as I'm concerned, you can go and take you a nap because there's nothing we need to talk about," Keisha replied and crossed her arms.

"I see your smart mouth hasn't changed and I'm not going anywhere until we do."

"Jessie, we have absolutely nothing to talk about unless you're gonna apologize."

"Apologize? For what?" Jessie asked as he raised his eyebrows in confusion. Keisha stood to her feet. She couldn't believe Jessie played the dumb role like he didn't know what she was talking about.

"Are you really serious right now? You know exactly what I'm talking about Jessie," Keisha explained. Jessie moved from where he stood to directly in front of her with a serious stone look on his face.

"Oh, I see someone is still living in the past. All that stuff happened a long time ago and I've moved on. Why can't you?"

"Excuse me? So you think I'm supposed to just move on and act like the molestation, the pregnancy never happened? Is that what I'm supposed to do?" Keisha inquired.

"There you go again, bringing up the past when that's where it should be left... the past. Bringing up the past is not healthy and it's also not biblical. We can't take anything that happened in the past back all we can do is try our best and move on. Come on Keisha, what would Jesus do?"
Keisha held up her hand to stop Jessie's bogus comment.

"Save your religion, Jessie. I can't believe you're standing here and try to deny all of the things you did to me and then put God up in it at the same time. Man, get outta here! What would Jesus do? Are you serious? Well since you want to stand there and throw it at me I might as well return the favor. Would Jesus sleep with little girls? Would he hold his nasty hands over their little mouth so that no one hears them? Don't you go there with me about what Jesus would do" Keisha replied. She could tell Jessie started to get angry by his stance.

"You know what? You're just like your..." Jessie caught himself before he finished his statement.

"What?" Keisha asked.

"Nothing. I find it quite odd that you want to pass judgment on me when you weren't a complete angel yourself. You were far from perfect too. I bet Alonzo and Kennedi still don't know about your stint in rehab and I'm definitely sure you didn't bother to mention anything about that to your precious husband."

"You're right. They don't know anything about what went on and I would like to keep it that way. And you better not say anything about it either. You've already caused me enough pain it's the least you can do."

"The only reason why you're still in pain is because you haven't moved on. You're still that same little angry girl that lived here years ago and I see nothing has changed."

"It's funny that after all these years you can't even say one simple word like sorry. You have to walk around here like some saint when I know that you're nothing but a well dressed devil. How about being sorry for screwing up my head and my life?"

"The only one responsible for screwing up your head and your life are you. Keisha everything you're talking about happened so many years ago. And, even if I did apologize, would you accept it?" Jessie asked then, when Keisha hesitated, he continued.

"My point exactly so why apologize for something I supposedly did to you and things are going to still be the same between us? So it really doesn't matter if I apologize right?"

Tears rolled down Keisha's face as she looked at Jessie. "I swear I hate you," Keisha said then made her way toward the steps. But, he got in the last word before she disappeared upstairs.

"Well, you can hate me all you want. If you desire to go to hell, that's your choice."

Keisha slammed her bedroom door and locked it. She didn't even comment on what her uncle said to her because she knew it was useless. Talking to Jessie was like trying to play a broken record. There was no point in it at all. Keisha even felt like she'd made a huge mistake in deciding to come home. She reached in her bag, tipped the prescription bottle in her hand, and decided she would sleep until it was time to leave.

# pretty skeletons

After that argument, Keisha packed up her duffle bag and sat on the porch waiting for Kennedi and Alonzo to come back. They weren't supposed to leave for an entire day but Keisha didn't care. As far as she was concerned, their little "visit" home was already over. Of course, her brother and sister tried to figure out what went on between them while they were out with Darlene but she didn't say anything. She just put her earphones on and turned her iPod up as high as it could go.

# chapter 12

Keisha sat at her desk, trying to complete some paperwork Michael gave her but found herself unable to concentrate. It had been three hours since he'd first handed it to her and, normally, she would've been done. However, she hadn't managed to complete a single thing. She flipped through the stack of paper aimlessly as her mind replayed the argument she had with Jessie.

She couldn't understand how one man could do so much evil over the years and never admit his wrongdoings. It angered her to think about all of the pain he caused her and how he turned the whole situation around to make it appear as her fault. The more she sat and thought about what happened over the weekend, the more upset she became. She reached underneath her desk for her purse. She unzipped her Coach bag and searched around for something she could take to calm her nerves but forgot she switched purses that morning.

Her office phone rang as she closed her handbag.

"Keisha, is that document I gave you ready to go?" Michael asked, snapping her back into reality for the task at hand.

"Umm, I'm almost finished with it and I'll have it done in the next fifteen minutes," Keisha lied. She knew fifteen minutes was pushing it to complete the paperwork but felt she had to say something. And she figured telling him she'd stared at it, did nothing for an entire hour, wasn't sufficient enough.

"That's fine. I need it before I leave in an hour."

"Okay, I'll have it to you by then," Keisha replied and placed the office phone on the receiver. An hour gave her plenty of time to have it done. Her phone vibrated twice to notify her thatshe had an appointment with Dr. Karen and a text message. She opened up her inbox and saw the message from Malik.

Malik: What's up Keesh?

She replied. Why are you texting me? LOL! Sike, I'm finishing up work and have an appointment.

Malik. That's too bad because I was gonna ask you out for lunch.

Keisha. Sorry, maybe next time.

Malik. Hey when you're free sometime, maybe you can stop by and check out my place one day.

Keisha. K, ttyl.

She laughed at Malik's random text. He always had a way of reaching out to her when she least expected it. But having the nerve to ask her to lunch, as if to suggest they go on a date while knowing her martial status, was a bit much. Then again, Malik's behavior didn't surprise her at all since he had a habit of doing exactly what he wanted to do regardless of what anyone said. And he'd always been that way.

Keisha took a deep breath and went on to finish her work before her boss left and in time to make her appointment with Dr. Karen.

From the moment Keisha paraded into her office, Karen picked up on the difference in her attitude but didn't say anything until she pressed the record button on the digital recorder.

"So, how are you coming along in progress since your last visit?" Dr. Karen asked. Keisha crossed her arms first, then her right leg over her left, and proceeded to roll her eyes.

"I'm not making progress at all," Keisha stated.

"Can you please elaborate?"

"Okay, the last time I was here, you told me how I should go home and confront him and try to deal with the issues from the past. That didn't do anything but make the entire situation worse!"

"Oh, so you did go home this past weekend? What happened? Please tell me about that."

"Well, first of all I was tricked into going home but that's beside the point. Once I got there, it was one thing after the other. Jessie really knows how to push my buttons."

"So, I'm guessing you two got into an argument?"

# pretty skeletons

"Huh? Did we? That's all we did. If we weren't, he was sliding in ignorant and inappropriate comments just like he did when I lived there. That man hasn't changed at all."

"But, at least you did get a chance to confront him. You, at the very least, accomplished that."

"As far as I'm concerned, that's not an accomplishment at all. It didn't do anything but make my situation worse. Interacting with him is like pulling a scab off an old wound and pouring alcohol in it then setting fire to it."

"And that's understandable. I told you, in your previous sessions, that going back and peeling off layers from the past is painful but necessary."

Keisha held up her hand to halt her therapist from saying anything else.

"I understand that you feel what you're telling me will help because you've learned it out of some textbook or something, but I really don't see how it's making things better. I want to tell you that this is my last session. I'm done!" Keisha pressed the stop button on the recorder and rose to her feet.

"Keisha, I know that going back into your past is painful but it's the only way I can truly help you. We have to revisit those painful memories in order to move on. Please... Don't leave!" Karen followed Keisha to the door.

"Look, I know you were only trying to help and I appreciate what you're trying to do but I'm finished with your services. Goodbye!" Keisha opened the door and excused herself before the doctor had a chance to respond. Keisha knew she shocked Karen by what she just did but felt it to be the best decision. Keisha really thought going through therapy would help her be able to feel better about the things she'd gone through, but it only seemed to make her feel horrible. And from the pit of her stomach, she believed the entire situation would get a whole lot worse before it got better.

By the time she reached her home, she found herself mentally exhausted. All she wanted to do was go upstairs, take a few pills, and climb in bed but knew the twins wouldn't allow her the luxury. She was surprised when she walked through the door and they weren't standing there to greet her.

"Hey honey, I'm glad you're home," David said as he met her at the door with a kiss.

"Hey babe," she replied and set her purse down on the center island in the kitchen. Keisha hoped he didn't pick up on her foul mood. She tried to shrug off the day's events but couldn't seem to shake her emotions.

"You had a long day?" David asked as he joined his wife at the kitchen table.

"Yeah, I guess you can say that," she answered. David probed deeper into her quick answer.

"You haven't said two words to me since you've come back from Columbus. Is everything okay, Keisha?"

"I'm okay. Why? Does it seem like something is wrong?"

"Yeah it does. That's why I decided to send the kids with your sister tonight. I've set up something to make you feel all better," he said.

"What are you talking about?" Keisha asked curiously. David let a sneaky smile creep across his face as he took her by the hand.

"Follow me."

He led her upstairs to their master suite where the lights were dim. Floetry's newest CD played softly in the background and he'd lit various fresh linen candles throughout the room.

"David, you didn't have to do this!" Keisha insisted as she took in the sensual ambiance of the room.

"Baby, I wanted to do something nice for you. You've been stressed lately and I know that it's hard dealing with the kids, work, and your uncle being sick."

"I told you I was okay. You certainly didn't have to go to all this trouble just for me."

"This wasn't any trouble at all. Besides, I love doing nice things for you so let me help you relax." David pulled her hair to the side and kissed her on the back of her neck. He then let his fingers travel down her body and removed her blouse over her head.

Usually, she would melt at her husband's touch. But, for some reason, she couldn't rid her mind of images of her Uncle Jessie and how he used to touch her in ways that made her feel dirtier than the bottom of a garbage truck.

# pretty skeletons

Keisha closed her eyes, hoping the flashbacks from her taunted past disappeared as fast as they come but they didn't. They kept flashing before her like she watched a movie. She breathed in and out, trying to relax, but that didn't do anything. She still stood frozen in position as he removed her clothing piece by piece. David then began to rub her back and, while the massage made her felt great, she still couldn't unwind. He moved her to their bed and, before she could protest, she became lost in his sweet, sensual, kisses. For a moment, it seemed to ease her from such silent torture until she opened her eyes and saw him.

"Stop it Jessie!" Keisha screamed and then looked up at her husband realizing what she actually said.

"What's wrong Keisha?" David asked as he rolled over to his side of the bed and sat up.

"Nothing. I just don't feel like it tonight. Okay?" Keisha responded.

"Something is wrong for sure. You just called me Jessie."

"No, I didn't." She insisted. She knew what she called him but tried to convince him otherwise and really didn't know how she could explain it to him.

"Either I'm hearing things or you don't know what you just said. But, you called me Jessie!"

"If I called you Jessie, I'm sorry. I just have a lot on my mind and going home to see him didn't make it any better."

"Do you want to finally talk about it? I'm here to listen."

"I really don't want to talk about anything. I would like to just put on my nightgown and go to sleep."

"But, babe, I ordered food from your favorite restaurant for dinner," David revealed.

"Just save it for me. I'll eat it tomorrow," Keisha said as she slipped on her oversized t-shirt and pulled back her side of the bed.

"So that's it? You're just gonna go to sleep? I had our whole night planned."

"I understand and I apologize for ruining it but I'm tired."

"Alright Keisha," David put on a sleeveless t-shirt, some basketball shorts, and went back downstairs. She knew she upset him by shutting down his entire romantic evening. She had never denied her husband sex the entire time they were married but it was the furthest thing from her mind that night. She knew him to be a very understanding man and, as she lay in bed alone, she hoped he continued to empathize with her.

Keisha woke up the next morning feeling horrible about the way she treated David. All he wanted to do was surprise her with a quiet, romantic evening at home and, once again she stopped that from happening. She knew she had to make it up to him somehow so, when she rolled over and saw him still lying in the bed, she decided to take the opportunity.

"Good morning, baby," Keisha sang and touched his shoulder, hoping to wake him up. When he didn't answer her back, she nudged him a little harder. He still didn't say anything. Keisha knew he would be upset but she didn't expect him to be mad to the point of not speaking to her. Just when she got ready to say something, he rolled over with a grimace fixated on his face.

"What's wrong with you? Are you still mad at me?"

"No, I'm not mad but can you go to the medicine cabinet and grab me one of my Vicodin?"

"Why? What's going on?"

"I don't' know. My back is hurting me. It all started when I was cutting hair at the shop yesterday. I thought it would go away but it's even worse now."

"Where's your pills at?" Keisha asked even though she already knew the answer.

"They should be in the cabinet on the left near the bottom." David moaned and tried to reposition himself to get comfortable.

"Okay, let me look." She walked into the bathroom, thankful David hadn't decided to get up and retrieve them himself. At least, this way, she could slip him one pill until she found away to replace the ones she'd taken. She took her time and closed the doors so he couldn't see her. She opened the cabinet and reached for the bottle of Vicodin and realized it was completely empty. There wasn't anything in the bottle but cotton. Keisha pulled it out, hoping a few pills got stuck, but nothing was there.

## pretty skeletons

Keisha paced back and forth in the bathroom, trying to figure out what she was going to do. There is no way I took an entire bottle of pills. I only remember popping a couple. She thought.

Keisha mentally retraced her steps to remember all the times she had indeed cracked the bottle open and only come up with three. What in the world am I going to tell David? Even if I come up with something, he's not going to believe me.

She opened up the trash can and tossed the empty bottle inside. Afterwards, she began making noise in the cabinet and moving things around.

"Baby, did you find them?" David called out.

Keisha opened the door. "I'm still looking. I don't see your pills anywhere."

"That's odd because I could've swore they were in the medicine cabinet last week."

"Well, I don't see them, honey. Are you sure you ordered some more?"

"Yeah, I thought I did but maybe I didn't."

"I'll continue to look if you want me to." Keisha started to walk back into the bathroom on another bogus search when he stopped her.

"Naw babe. Just give me a couple of Tylenols and call the shop and tell the guys I won't be coming in today?"

"Sure thing!" Keisha breathed out a sigh of relief for missing the near bullet as she remained in denial about consuming his entire bottle of pills. A handful of them had to have fallen out somewhere. She made a mental note to check her bags once David wasn't around.

Her phone vibrated while she poured him a glass of water. She pressed the button to retrieve a message.

Malik. What's up Keesh?

She shook her head and rolled her eyes.

Keisha. Why are you texting me?

Malik. You can be so cold sometimes. LOL… What are you doing?

Keisha. Minding my business… Something you should try.

Malik. If we didn't have so much history, I would've called you all kinds of expletives by now.

---

# JESSICA A. ROBINSON

Keisha. Ooh, did you look that one up in the dictionary?

Malik. Anyways, what are you doing later? And before you shut me down, be honest because we need to talk.

Keisha. Talk about what?

Malik. Don't worry about it. Just answer my question.

Keisha. Not too much of anything. My sister has my kids and my husband isn't feeling well. He's in bed...

Malik. Well, how about you meet me over my place in a half hour. Can you make that happen?

Keisha. Umm, I don't know.

Malik. My address is 6247 Sleeping Willows Dr. I would say I'll see you in a half hour but, with your attitude, I'll give you an extra half hour. LOL.

Keisha. Whatever Malik...goodbye.

She laughed and placed her cell phone on vibrate. Malik could be so bossy sometimes and down right hard headed when it came to getting what he wanted. He was one of those people who never took no for an answer.

Once she took a shower, she put on her gray BeBe jogging suit then went into the bedroom to check on David. Since the Tylenol 3's he had taken earlier had him in a full fledge snore, she figured she wouldn't wake him. She found a piece of paper nearby and wrote him a short note:

*Hey baby,*
*I had to run out to the store. If you need anything, please call.*
*I love you,*
*Keisha*

After Keisha wrote her husband the note, she got in her car and took the twenty-five minute drive to Malik's house.

What do you want? Keisha asked as she glanced at her phone and saw that it was Jessie's number. She was almost at Malik's house and had been listening to Keyshia Cole's CD, A Different Me. She didn't know what it was but something about that CD always helped her to loosen up. However, it all flew out the window when he called. "Keisha, that's not a way to greet someone on the phone," Jessie warned her as if he tried to scold her.

# pretty skeletons

"I'll talk to you however I want. You called my phone." Keisha's nostrils began to flare as she answered him. She could feel herself getting angry and he hadn't even said two sentences to her.

"Listen, I'm not calling to engage in this devilish conversation you're choosing to have with me. I called so we could bury the hatchet."

"Bury what hatchet? You meant to say everything you said to me when I was there."

"No, I didn't. I really didn't mean those evil things. It was my mistake."

"Well, the only mistake I made was coming home to see you. I'll bury the hatchet if I can stab you in the back with it first!"

"Keisha, I understand you're upset but can we at least let this go and put last weekend behind us? That's what God would want us to do."

"Oh, so you're calling to preach to me?"

"Well, someone needs to. You can't possibly be mad and hate me forever."

"Yes I can! Watch me!" Keisha pressed the end button on her phone and pulled into Malik's driveway. She parked behind a brand new Black Jaguar XF that still had its thirty day tag on it. She honestly didn't know how she even made it to Malik's house without getting lost. She had been so consumed with Jessie that she didn't remember driving through his neighborhood at all.

Malik's front door consisted of a design made completely of decorative glass. As soon as she stepped upon the porch, he met her.

"I'm glad you didn't stand me up."

"You said you needed to talk so that's why I'm here," Keisha answered in an irritated tone. Malik jumped back like she spit fire from her mouth and he wasn't trying to get burned. He stepped to the side and let Keisha enter into his foyer.

"Sounds like someone has pissed you off..."

"Jessie called me."

"I see he still has the ability to take you there." Malik closed his front door and led her into his living room.

143

"Of course, I still can't stand the ground he walks on but that's a never ending battle. I didn't come all the way over here to talk about him, though. What did you want?" Keisha asked, hoping to shift their conversation fast and in a hurry before she caught an attitude all over again.

"First, before we talk, I would like to take you on a tour of my home."

"That's fine."

He walked her around the main level, showing her the formal living room, dining room, family room with the wrap around kitchen she'd only previously seen on the television, and the first class professional studio he installed himself. He then took her upstairs and showed her each one of the three bedrooms that appeared to be mini suites of their own. The last thing he revealed was the master bedroom. The moment he opened the double doors, it amazed her.

"Wow! You definitely saved the best for last. This is really nice. You set this up all by yourself?"

"No, I wish I could take the credit but I hired an interior decorator to complete the entire house."

"That's nice. And I'm so glad you didn't take it upon yourself to decorate because you would've had this place looking like a circus." Keisha laughed and Malik rolled his eyes at her.

"Whatever! I have impeccable taste." He popped the collar on his navy blue button down Sean John as if he proclaimed some great truth.

"So, I take it that's your brand new Jag sitting in the driveway too." Keisha crossed her arms over her chest.

"I just drove off the car lot three days ago with that."

"Okay, so you have this brand new house, a brand new Jag, a BMW, and you're hiring decorators. That's not cheap. What's up?"

Malik raised his eyebrows in confusion. "What do you mean what's up?"

"I know you have the hair salon and stuff. You're the sole owner but how are you doing all this on that type of money?" Keisha was curious as to how Malik owned a house that was nothing short of a masterpiece and two of the most expensive cars on the market. Something just didn't add up to her. Even though Malik was an entrepreneur like her husband they lived comfortably in comparison to his extravagance. "You probably think I'm still out on the block to be rolling like I am but I'm not. This is all legit. My business is doing well. Besides, being out on the streets is old anyway."

Keisha had to do all she could to keep from laughing. She had heard a whole bunch of lies and had a feeling he just told one.

"Was something I said funny to you?" Malik asked as they walked down the steps and back into the living room.

"I guess you can say I'm just a little bit tickled to hear you confess to me that you're done with the streets. When you were younger, you said you'd be on the block until the day you stopped breathing."

"I know that's what I said but I was young and dumb. Since then, I realized I had to move on to bigger and better things. Enough about me! I didn't bring you over here to discuss all that but I did think we needed to talk though," Malik uttered and motioned for her to join him on the tan and brown couch.

"About what?" Keisha inquired.

"Well, Alonzo was over here the other day and we got to talking. He ended up telling me about you and Jessie getting into it over the weekend when you went home."

Here we go again, she thought. Just when she tried to forget about the very person who sent her blood pressure to dangerously high levels, he somehow came up again. She couldn't understand why her brother told Malik her business. She knew Malik was his best friend but she believed some things should be kept within their family. The only reason why Keisha didn't get too upset was because, next to her diary, Malik practically knew everything that happened to her while she lived with Jessie and Darlene. He was the shoulder she cried on and the person she trusted with all of her deepest, darkest secrets. Even though he had been out on the streets selling drugs and heavy in the dope game, he was the only person who understood her the most. That made them stick closer than glue when she was in high school and also the very same reason she became hooked on prescription pills.

"Yeah, Jessie and I got into it. I wish I never even went home with them."

"Zoe never told me but what did y'all argue about?"

"What don't we argue about? We argue because he's still the same low down dirty bastard he was when I was a little girl," Keisha fumed. Her chest rose and fell as she paused.

"So, he hasn't changed at all?"

"Please, that man ain't never gonna change. He's still evil and praises his God at the same time."

"Man, that's crazy Keesh. So you two have never settled all of that stuff that went on back in the day?"

"Not at all. As far as he is concerned, nothing happened between me and him. He told me in so many words that I'm going to hell because I haven't forgiven him but he can save all of it for someone who really cares. If I'm going to hell, then he'll definitely be going there before I do," Keisha smacked her lips.

"Wow, well since you know he's still up to no good, maybe you can just go your separate ways."

"Malik, I tried that. But now, Darlene and Jessie call my house, my cell phone. And when I don't answer or hang up on them, they send their little messages thru Zoe or Kennedi. It's like they exist to make my life a living hell!"

"Humph! That's a trip!" Malik shook his head back and forth, not knowing what else to say.

"I've been stressed out. Can't sleep. Been acting different around my husband. I'm completely on edge."

"Well, have you ever told your husband about all of this? Maybe you need to go and get some professional help or somethin."

"No, he doesn't know anything about my past and I want to keep it that way. And, I went to a therapist. I'm sorry, instead of things getting better, they're getting worse!"

"So you're telling me your husband doesn't know about your past at all?"

"No, he doesn't know. He knows nothing about the molestation, my addiction, or rehab. He just knows that I don't get along with Jessie."

# pretty skeletons

"Wow! So I know if he doesn't know, you still haven't told your brother or sister."

"Hold up. Why are we playing twenty one questions? Can I use your bathroom over there?" Keisha asked, pointing to the half bathroom in the foyer.

"Oh, don't use that bathroom! I forgot to replace the light bulbs. Use the one in my bedroom."

Keisha made a dash upstairs and was glad to have escaped Malik's questioning for a moment. She knew he was generally concerned about her but it seemed like, when she tried to move on from the issues bothering her, there was always something or someone to draw her right back in the middle of it all. She could feel her head pounding and she knew she would end up having a headache. For a moment, she thought about searching in her purse for any loose pills that may have fallen out but had already looked there before she left the house. After she used the bathroom and washed her hands, she splashed some water on her face. She didn't know how much longer she could go on without having a steady flow of pills. Keisha opened up Malik's medicine cabinet, hoping to find some Tylenol, but ended up stumbling upon an entire cupboard full of prescription pills. She pulled out a few bottles to look at them. When she saw that each one contained a different name, she realized Malik was indeed still in the game. She always knew Malik like the back of her hand and she wasn't shocked to be right on.

# chapter 13

Keisha walked through the front door of her home to find her husband sitting on the couch watching ESPN.

"I'm glad to see you out of the bed," she smiled and set her Target bags down near the base of the steps. He picked up the remote and pressed the mute button.

"I feel like a new man, baby. That medicine you gave me worked. Even though it wasn't what I usually take, it still did the job." David held his arms out and Keisha bent down and kissed him.

"I'm glad you're feeling better. I was worried about you while I was out at the store."

"I appreciate your concern but you know how my back gets sometimes. I've looked for my prescription high and low and I haven't found them at all. That bothers me 'cause I could've sworn they were in the bathroom where I always keep them."

"You still haven't found them?" Keisha asked with a clueless disposition.

"No, baby, there's no trace of them at all. But, it's cool because I contacted my doctor and he called in another prescription at the pharmacy so I'll be okay for a while," he explained.

Keisha responded, "Good babe. I'm glad you got everything worked out."

The next morning Keisha woke up before the sun made its grand appearance in the sky. By the time her husband and twins made it to breakfast, she had already washed four loads of laundry, cleaned the entire house, and picked the twins school outfits. David stood in the corner of the kitchen and watched his wife serve the children breakfast, moving back and forth in the kitchen as if she competed in a race against time. He chuckled and crossed his arms over his muscular chest as he observed her behavior.

"Looks like someone is in a good mood this morning. How long have you been up?"

"I've been up since four. I know that's pretty early but I figured I'd wake up and do some things around the house before everyone got up. Just tryin' to stay ahead of things," Keisha replied, talking with the speed of an announcer at an auction.

"Okay honey, whatever you say. Breakfast smells good!" David smiled as Keisha put a crescent shaped omelet on a plate and handed it to him.

"I made your favorite."

"Okay, is everything fine with you? It seems like something is going on."

"No, everything is fine. Why would you say that?" Keisha looked surprised as she joined him at the table with their kids.

"Well, I always associate my favorite omelet with your way to make up with me, as sort of peace offering. Remember the last time you fixed me breakfast like this?" David asked and then stuffed a fork full into his mouth.

Keisha pressed her lips together and shook her head, acknowledging what he said. Of course, she remembered the last time she fixed him such an elaborate breakfast - she had maxed out his American Express Card. She hardly ever ran up the charges on his credit cards but Saks Fifth Avenue had a sale in addition to MAC releasing their new make up collection.

"Yeah, I remember. But I promise, it's nothing like that. I just wanted to do something nice for you this morning. Is that a crime?"

"No, it's not but if it turns out that his meal was a cover up for something else, I'm going to bring up this conversation," David laughed.

"I promise you. It's not."

Keisha loaded her kids in the car and drove all the way to their school with a grin on her face. She even walked into work smiling and humming a song. She was in a great mood thanks to the couple of Vicodin pills she took when she woke up that morning. They proved to be the very thing she needed to maintain her motivation as they definitely improved her mood and allowed her to get some work done.

When Michael came through the double glass doors of the law firm, like he always does in the middle of the morning, Keisha had already completed the pile of paperwork he had left her the night before and had provided him with a list of her own. He was taken by surprise. "Wow, I surely thought it would take until lunch to finish what I gave you."

"I had a feeling that your caseload picked up so I decided to come in a little earlier and try to get everything done." Keisha flashed her infectious smile which caused her boss to change his emotionless countenance.

"Well, you've done a great job. I'll have all the necessary documents you requested by lunchtime," Michael said, bowing his head in appreciation. She laughed and responded.

"Thanks Michael."

Keisha could hear her phone vibrating in her purse inside her desk. She opened the drawer and glanced at it. She realized she had three missed calls and a text message from Malik. She opened up her inbox and read his message.

Keisha I've been trying to reach you and you seem to be avoiding me. I need to see you ASAP. Malik.

Keisha locked her cell phone and placed it back inside her purse. She really didn't desire to talk to Malik, figuring she would call him when she got good and ready. She knew Malik really didn't want anything so he would just have to catch her when he could. For the next hour and a half, she tried to make herself busy and catch up on updating some files but her phone continued to vibrate. And when she thought it stopped, it vibrated again. She grew irritated with Malik blowing up her phone. He didn't show any signs of ceasing to call her so she decided to answer.

"Hello? What's up? You've been trying to reach me?" Keisha asked as she increased the volume on her phone.

"Keesh, this is Zoe. Malik's been tryin' to get a hold of you. Since you're not picking up your phone, he's callin' me. What's up?"

"I haven't been picking up because I'm obviously at work."

"I know but he's still wondering why you won't even text him back."

"Oh, it's cool. I'll just call him when I get done."

"I think he said he's going to stop by your job before you get off," Alonzo announced and then asked. "Are we all still meeting Eric for dinner tonight?"

"Yeah bro. Seven o'clock on the dot. See you later." Just then Keisha saw the double doors open and Malik stood before her own eyes.

"Zoe, I'll call you back later," Keisha uttered.

"Hey Malik, what are you doing here?" Keisha inquired, surprised to see him. She tried to contain the sudden nervousness that crept up in her tone. She hoped Malik didn't sense it at all.

"Come on, Keesh. You know exactly what I'm here so quit trying to act like you don't," Malik replied without even flashing a smile.

"Yeah, I know why you're here," Keisha answered as she looked down the hall to make sure Michael didn't come out of his office. She was somewhat relieved when she heard him shut his office door. Malik crossed his arms before he continued.

"So, why am I here?" He awaited her response.

"Let me guess. You're here because you missed me?" Keisha nervously chuckled.

"Guess again, Keisha," he glared. She just shrugged her shoulders.

"You know what? I don't know why you would be stopping here and you know I'm working."

"Okay, I see this isn't going to be easy. Since you've chosen to play the clueless role, let me refresh your memory. I've been missing something since you visited me."

"And what could that possibly be?" Keisha asked.

Malik lowered his voice to almost a whisper before he answered her. "Ten Vicodin pills and you know it so quit the games."

Keisha was surprised by Malik's accuracy. But then again, when it came to drugs and collecting his money, he became witty as an investment banker. With the dozens of pill bottles in his medicine cabinet, she thought she could slip a hand full without him even noticing but, apparently, Malik was like a watchdog over his empire.

"You're missing ten pills? That's ridiculous! Ain't nobody steal no ten pills from you!"

"Keisha, I know you did it. I sent you to the second floor bathroom on purpose. The one on the main level worked just fine." Malik crossed his arms and stared at Keisha who didn't know what to say at this point. She was busted. There was nothing else she could deny or play stupid about.

"So, you set me up?"

"Naw, I wouldn't say I set you up. But, I knew deep down inside you were on pills again," Malik replied and Keisha glanced back down the hall at Michael's shut door.

"You                don't                know                anything."

"Oh, I don't know anything, huh? Well, I know enough to know that you're back on pills. Look at you, acting all fidgety and nervous. I see it in your eyes!"

"Malik, I swear you don't know what you're talking about. You're fishin' for something."

Malik ignored her comment. "Do you know how much you owe me for those Vicodins?"

"Beats me because I didn't take them."

"Ten pills, I could've easily made three hundred, especially from someone who wants them bad enough."

"Well, I'm sorry that your inventory is a little off. Maybe you need to recount them 'cuz they might not be missing at all."

"I'd hate to have to call Zoe to settle this debt, considering he doesn't even know you're addicted in the first place." Malik pulled out his Palm Pre phone and acted as though he dialed Alonzo's number.

"You wouldn't."

"Keisha, you know I wouldn't want to do that but you're messin' with business and my livelihood. All I'm asking you to do is own up."

Keisha didn't want to admit the fact that she'd taken a few pills while she was at Malik's. She doesn't know where he got the number ten from. He exaggerated. She only remembered taking a few out of the bottle, not ten. But even though she didn't want to confess, Malik left her without a choice. She definitely didn't want her brother to find out so he forced her to keep it real with him.

"Okay, I did take them but I planned on hittin' you with some money for them. I'm still faced with a dilemma, though" Keisha said as she gave him a grave look.

"And what's that?"

"Out of the few I took from you, I only have three left. I'm gonna need some more before the day is over."

"No Keisha! Absolutely not! I already know what you're trying to imply and it's not happening."

"Why not Malik? I guess I could still be in denial but, the fact is, I'm back on pills and I know I'm gonna constantly need more. Now, whether I get them from you or someone else, I'm still going to need them."

All Malik could do was shake his head at her request. "I'm really not trying to go there with you," Malik insisted.
Keisha reached in her Coach purse, pulled out two hundred dollars, and gave it to him.

"I know you said three. I'll have the rest to you by tomorrow. If you'll excuse me, I need to get back to work."

If Malik wasn't going to agree to give her what she wanted, then she felt they had no other reason to talk. Malik recounted the money and then looked at Keisha.

"What's all this for?" he asked.

"You said I owed you three so that's two hundred of it," Keisha replied and rolled her eyes at him. Instead of putting the money in his pocket, he peeled off five twenties and handed the rest back to her. She had a confused look on her face but, before she could ask him what he was doing, he answered her.

"Here's some of your money back. I said I probably could've got three hundred but I wouldn't have gotten it like that."

Keisha let a smile slowly creep across her face. "So does this mean what I think it means?"

"Against my better judgment, yes. Keesh, when you need some, just hit me up. I gotta get out of here but, before I do, I just wanna tell you I hope I'm not making a mistake."

"Don't worry, you're not."

# pretty skeletons

Keisha watched as Malik exited the building and got into his Jaguar. Malik may have not known it but he made her the happiest woman in the world at that moment.

"I can't believe we're all together again. It's definitely been a while," Eric said as he walked up to the table in Beni-hana's to greet Keisha, David, Alonzo, and Kennedi.

"Yeah, it's definitely been a while. How you been?" Kennedi asked with pure lust in her voice and eyes. She looked at their old neighbor like he was one hundred percent pure Angus beef and stared like she was casting the role of baby daddy number two.

"I'm good. No complaints thus far, God has been good to me." Eric smiled revealing his boyish dimples. Kennedi returned the gesture and replied.

"He sure has."

Keisha observed the way her sister acted and cut in their conversation.

"I'm so sorry Eric. I didn't get a chance to introduce you to my husband David." The two men reached across the table and shook hands.

"I've heard so much about you. It's so nice to finally meet you," Eric said as Kennedi rolled her eyes quickly at her sister who silently laughing back at her.

"Nice to meet you, Eric. Keisha told me so many stories about you guys when you were little."

"Well, I wonder if she told you how greedy of a girl she used to be, eating up all the food my mother used to cook." He started to laugh.

"Eric, don't start. I'm not in the mood to embarrass you," Keisha replied.

"Sooooo... Keisha tells me you've been in Akron for a little while because of your job," Alonzo said while Kennedi appeared as if the words were literally taken right out of her mouth.

"Yeah, I have about three weeks left to train the rest of the staff then its back home to Pittsburgh."

"Man, that's what's up. You must've had a pretty high position to be traveling across the country to train people?"

Eric smiled and replied, "I'm not even gonna lie. I've worked hard to get where I am and where I am is all because of God."

"So, you're successful and humble about it. Umph... Umph... Umph," Kennedi said as she shook her head and smiled at Eric with a puppy dog look in her eyes. Keisha lightly kicked her and Kennedi cut her eyes, apparently catching an attitude.

"Well, I tell you what, you're wife and children are lucky to have a man like you," Kennedi continued, fishing for information despite her sister and brother's attempts to stop her.

"Oh, your sister didn't tell you? I'm single. No kids and no wife," he stated. Keisha noticed her sister's smile grew even wider but Eric's cell phone rang and he excused himself from the table. Alonzo and Keisha waited for him to walk out of hearing range of their conversation before they even spoke.

"Are you forgetting you have a boyfriend at home or what?" Alonzo asked.

"Zoe, I haven't forgotten anything. I know Quincy is at home."

"Well, I surely can't tell by the way you're flirting with him," he said as Kennedi returned the favor and rolled her eyes.

"Is it a crime that I'm flirting and being friendly with him? Shoot, the way I see it Eric is just the type of man that I need in my life. I can get rid of this loser of a person that I call my man."

"Hey sis, remember, he's your loser," Keisha laughed.

"Very funny Keesh. You know what I mean though. Alright, let's talk about something else because here he comes," Kennedi announced as she put back on her Colgate smile and forgot what they even said.

"I'm so sorry for running out like that. I had an important phone call. What did I miss?"

"You didn't miss anything. We were just talking about if your mom was here then everything would really be perfect. We would love to see Ms. Gina," Keisha said as she watched Kennedi breathe a sigh of relief.

"I know, right?" Eric asked then looked off in the distance and Ms. Gina walked into the restaurant smiling from ear to ear.

# pretty skeletons

"Did I just hear someone wanted to see me?" She smiled and everyone's mouth dropped open.

"Wow, Ms. Gina I cannot believe it's you," Alonzo rose to his feet and walked around the table to hug her. Her arms were open wide and she embraced him. Kennedi and Keisha got up as well but the last person to hug Gina was Keisha. She couldn't even speak because she was so choked up with emotion.

"It's okay Keisha, I'm so happy to finally see you."

"I thought I would never see you again."

"Even though we spent many years apart, I knew that God would allow us to cross paths."

Keisha couldn't believe she stood face to face with the woman who was responsible for raising her and her siblings for a period of time. Out of all of the women figures in her life, she loved Gina like her own mother. It was the type of bond she shared with Cecilia but somewhat deeper because of Gina's presence early on in her childhood.

When her mother passed, she honestly believed they would just live with Ms. Gina next door and pick up where they left but Darlene and Jessie appeared out of thin air to take all three of them in to their home. She remembered how thankful she was to have family who stepped up to the plate and raised them but, if she would've had the foresight to see what would happen once she moved with them, she would've begged to be placed in the foster care system.

"You look just like I remembered," Keisha said as she motioned for all of them to sit down.

"Aww, you're trying to make this old lady smile. You all look wonderful too," Gina replied and took her seat next to Eric.

"So you were planning this reunion this whole time huh?" Keisha asked.

"Yeah, I figured it was about time we all got back together. The whole eastside crew back in the same place, just like old times," Eric boasted.

"Yeah this feels just like old times. The only thing we're missing is your food Ms. Gina," Kennedi stated and winked at Eric who smiled back at her.

"Well, that can be arranged since we all don't live that far away from each other now. When I move into my new place, we can have a big dinner party at my house."

"Oooh, sounds like a plan." Alonzo rubbed his stomach and started to laugh because it growled.

After they placed their food and drink orders, they all caught up with each other discussing things that had gone after they had left and talked about the things currently happening.

"Wow, I can't believe you all have children. That's so wonderful. And Keisha, you and your husband make a lovely couple," Gina said.

David and Keisha smiled at each other and then thanked her.

"So, Eric told me he's been attending this lovely church while he's been here. I think he said the name is The House of the Lord. Is that the church you all attend?"

"No ma'am. We've been there and that is a great church but we go to New Word Christian Center. It's been my family's place of worship since I was a little boy."

"Oh that's good. I'm just glad you all still go to church. That was something that I always prayed about. That you three would remain going to church."

David raised his eyebrows and looked over at his wife.

"You used to go to church with Ms. Gina? I thought you told me that the first time you ever stepped foot in a church was with your aunt and uncle?" He looked at her confused and she offered the same puzzled look in return.

"You know what? I did tell you that. I'm sorry. Yeah, we used to attend church with them all the time."

"Oh okay," David answered and sat back in his chair a little.

"I remember we promised to write each other and that definitely never happened. I used to think you guys moved across the country and we lost touch forever," Keisha changed the subject. Ms. Gina looked over at Eric who glanced back at his mom in a perplexed manner.

"Keisha, you never got any of our letters?" she asked.
She shook her head no as she peered at her siblings who also shook their heads in unison.

# pretty skeletons

"No what letters?" Keisha inquired.

"The letters I used to make Eric write to you every week. We started about a month after you guys moved. I would also write a note with a scripture and send it to your aunt's house in Columbus. We kept writing until Eric turned sixteen. When we didn't hear anything back from you, we stopped but I still would send you guys a few lines every couple months to check on you," Gina explained.

"Wow," Keisha said. She was at a true loss of words.

"There obviously had to be some kind of mix up Ms. Gina because, if they came in the mail, Uncle Jessie would have passed them along to us. Maybe you had the wrong address or something," Alonzo replied, justifying the supposed mishap. But, Keisha felt deep down in her heart there was something foul about the situation. She didn't doubt the fact they sent mail for three years but did doubt that Jessie would give them the letters.

He probably opened the mail and destroyed it before she could even see it. He really didn't want them to have any contact with people from their old neighborhood. Keisha tried to keep up with a few friends she used to go to school with on the phone but, once he'd gotten wind of it, she received a lecture. He thoroughly explained to her that it wasn't beneficial for her to have any contact with the people who a part of her old life. And, since she'd moved to Columbus, she should concentrate on having new friends. Even after their talk, Keisha tried to still sneak on the phone with them until Jessie caught her and banned her from the privilege all together. She didn't want to press the issue any further and decided to just go along with him to make her life a little easier.

# chapter 14

"Mommy, when you pick us up from school, can we go to McDonald's to get a Happy Meal?" D.J. asked as Keisha drove away from their subdivision.

"D.J., I don't want to go to McDonald's. I want to eat sloppy joes and fries," Katrina announced.

"Well, I want McDonald's."

"Sloppy joes."

"McDonald's!"

"Sloppy joes!"

"Listen, if you two don't shut up then you're not gonna eat anything. Now, sit back in your seat and shut your mouths! We're almost at school!" Keisha explained as she stared at them through her rearview mirror. She was completely on edge and had been rushing the entire morning since she woke up late. If she had to actually work that day, she would've been later than usual and behind. Fortunately, she was off.

She'd set her alarm clock to wake her up in enough time to get the kids ready but, by the time she heard it sounding off, she had already set herself back thirty-minutes. It usually never took her that long to wake up but she'd endured a horrible night. She went to sleep like normal but found herself tossing and turning, having nightmares about Jessie being in their house. For close to three hours, she struggled to shut her eyes. When that didn't work, she hit her stash up and took a couple of pills which inevitably did the trick. However, the very thing to put her to sleep was the same thing to blame for her tardiness that morning. She was in such a rush she didn't even get a chance to take a couple before she left the house, which contributed to her sudden short fuse.

"Mommy, we're sorry," Katrina said as she stared at Keisha with a sad look. She usually could get out of any

---

161

trouble she was in with that look but on this particular morning Keisha wasn't buying that. Not at all.

"I have told you two, repeatedly, about all this bickering and fighting. I'm getting sick of it! And, if it continues, I'm gonna start poppin' y'all," Keisha replied as she watched both of her children lower their heads as if accused of committing a crime.

"Okay Mommy. We won't fight," D.J. said as she cut her eyes at him instead of responding.

"Mom, are you okay?" Katrina asked as she studied her mother's expressions.

"Yeah honey. I'm fine. Why?" Keisha pulled in the circular driveway of the elementary school and put the car in park.

"I don't know. It seems like you're mad."

Keisha softened the tension in her face and offered a smile.

"No. I'm okay, honey. Mommy's just a little tired. That's all. Now, I want you and your brother to have a good day at a school." Keisha reached out to hug and kiss them before they exited the car. They felt at ease as they walked toward the doors of the building. She was glad she could put a smile on their face before they left. She hadn't planned on snapping at them but also hadn't expected them to be arguing so early in the morning.

Keisha went to pull away when a little boy ran in front of her car. She pumped of her brakes and the frightened little boy ran into the school. She shook her head and wished she had extra time because she would have definitely tracked him down and gave him a spanking to remember. It irritated her when children paid no attention to their surroundings and placed themselves in all kinds of danger without realizing it.

Just as she got ready to drive off for the second time, she noticed her diary sticking out from underneath the passenger's seat. How in the world did my diary get there? I thought it was in my purse at home. She thought.

She, then, remembered the day she walked out on Dr. Karen and how she threw it in the car because she'd left in such a hurry. Keisha picked it back up and flipped through its worn contents. She thought about her conversations with Dr. Karen when she saw her on a regular basis and how she told her that,

## pretty skeletons

in order to heal the present, she had to be willing to go into the past. But, reaching back seemed to hurt more than it helped and going back in time contributed to her present state.

Before she could make it back home, David called her to come to the shop. Keisha entered just as he finished cutting his business partner's, father's hair. She walked right up to him and kissed him. The simple gesture produced an immediate smile on his face.

"Baby, why don't Jaime cut his own father's hair?" Keisha asked as she stared at the man walking out the shop. David brushed the hair that had fallen into his barber chair onto the floor.

"He said his son doesn't know what he's doing and I cut it just the way he likes it," David smiled as Jaime smacked his lips.

"Shut up David! Why you lying to Keesh like that?" he said as he tossed some balled up paper in David's direction. David erupted in laughter.

"Bay, let me stop lying. His dad came to me for a cut because Jaime was busy with a client and my first client cancelled."

"Thank you," Jaime answered.

"You and Jaime stay fighting with each other, huh?"

"We wouldn't have it any other way. Oh, before I forget, I need you to do me a huge favor."

"What you need, honey?" Keisha asked as she watched her husband reach in his back pocket and pull out some money.

"Can you stop by and pay the electric bill for me? I was gonna pay it later but I forgot today is my late day here at the shop." David counted out two hundred dollars and handed it to Keisha.

"You want me to pay this now?"

"Yeah. I was supposed to pay it last week but we should be fine because we're never late."

She shook her head at his request and stuffed the currency into her right jeans' pocket. "Alright babe, I'm going to get out of here and let you back to work. I'll take care of it." Keisha left the barbershop with one the thing and one thing only on her mind – to pay the electric bill with the money he gave her.

She knew she needed to apply it to for the account rather than hold the money in her pocket. Lord knows what she would do if she held onto it. When she arrived at the electric company, it surprised her to be able to park right in front of the building. Usually, so many different people running in and out made it almost impossible to find a spot so close. Keisha parallel parked against the curb and pressed her car alarm button. She walked up the six steps leading to the front door and almost knocked someone down while she going through the door.

"I'm sorry. I didn't see you when I opened the door," Keisha said as she looked up and discovered Malik in front of her. "Malik?"

"You better be glad you bumped into me. If it had been somebody else, they would've been ready to fight!" He laughed as he motioned for her to step to the side and allow an elderly woman to pass.

"Okay, so now I really think you're following me. Do you have a tracking device on my car?"

"Funny, real funny. If you haven't noticed, this is Ohio Edison. I had to pay Mr. Electric a visit just like you." Malik pointed down to the bill she held tightly.

She couldn't argue. They were both at a common public place and didn't know that each would be there. It was pure coincidence.

"Well, if you'll excuse me, I gotta go." Keisha went to turn around and walk away from Malik but he held onto her arm.

"Yo, Keesh, do you need some more paper 'cuz I got a fresh supply in the car if you do," he said as he winked. Keisha knew exactly what was trying to say.

"Ummm… yeah. I do need some more paper. Can I go in here real quick and then I'll be right out."

Malik glanced down at this diamond Rolex watch. "That's the thing Keesh. If you want it, you got to come now because I have somewhere I need to be." Malik looked down at the time again and then crossed his arms. He stood there patiently waiting for her answer. She mentally debated back and forth, in need of some pills in the worst way, but she knew her husband sent her down there to pay their electric bill. She reached in her purse trying to find he money she'd previously set aside to pay

Malik but forgot she's spent it on miscellaneous items at Target.

Keisha reached in her jean pocket and took out the money David gave her. Without putting too much more thought into the whole scenario, she inhaled then proceeded with a huge sigh.

"Okay Malik. Let me get some of that paper," Keisha replied and followed suite behind him out of the building.

A week later, Keisha was contacted by her therapist's secretary. She stated that Dr. Karen wanted to meet with her one more time if she would agree to it. Against her better judgment, she decided to go. So, she sat face to face, with Karen, sweating like she stole something and more nervous than ever. She took some pills before she left the house and sipped on some Hennessey, hoping to calm her nerves. But, for some odd reason, it made her feel even more anxious. She tried to be on her best behavior so Karen wouldn't pick up on the fact she was slightly drunk.

"I must admit. When I called, I didn't expect to hear anything back from you at all. I'm glad you came," Dr. Karen said as she closed her office door. Keisha sat in her usual spot on the couch. She honestly thought she'd never find herself in the office again.

"Well, you know me. I'm always full of surprises," Keisha said as she burped. She placed a hand over her mouth and replied, "Excuse me. Must be something I ate."

"It's okay. I know you're probably wondering why I called you to come in but I felt it was necessary to complete an evaluation, especially since you've opted out of treatment."

"What? You mean you didn't have me come in because I won a prize? Huh?" Keisha asked and then started to laugh at her own comment.

"Sorry, Keisha, no gifts here. But, I do want to talk about your progress since the last time your last visit."

"Progress? Hmmmm… Let's see. Things are still the same. Ain't nothing changed. I was a fool to think reading from that stupid notebook would help me."

"So nothing's changed?"

"Absolutely not. Well, things have changed but for the worse. I regret even digging back into my past. It's not even like I'm even surprised honestly. It's the story of my life," Keisha explained. She sat across from Dr. Karen tapping her leg on the floor, awaiting Karen's response. Instead, Dr. Karen just sat quietly and watching. Keisha rocked back and forth in her seat and burped a few times.

"Keisha, is that alcohol I smell on you?" Dr. Karen sniffed.

"Yeah why?"

"Since when did you start drinking? In one of our beginning sessions, you told me you weren't a drinker."

"I know what I said but I didn't say I may consume a drink from time to time. It's a lot of things that I swore to myself I would never do but things just happen I guess. I mean look at my history with prescription pills. I remember being a little girl and watching my mother so high on crack and I used to tell myself that I would never ever touch anything that was considered a drug and look at me. I ended up in rehab before I even turned eighteen. So like I said we may say a lot of things that we may never do but some things are beyond our control."

"Okay, I can understand certain things being out of our control but not everything is a direct result of being powerless. We do have some control on how we handle certain things. I just find it odd that you're drinking at such an odd hour."

"Oh well, I felt the need to sip on a little something before I came to see you. It has calmed my nerves considerably." Keisha said, actually trying to believe it herself because she was more uptight than ever.

"Keisha, what's really going on?"

"What do you mean?"

"Something is definitely going on with you. I'm concerned for you, Keisha. Not only as your therapist but as your friend."

"Don't be concerned about me, Dr. Karen. I'll be fine. Besides, all the damage to my life has already been done. I really don't think it would get any worse."

Keisha knew that was crazy to admit but felt it was the truth. She already considered her life to be in shambles and, even though Dr. Karen appeared to have the cement glue that could attempt to put it back together, she didn't believe it could be fixed. There wasn't really anyone she felt could fix the problems embedded deep inside of her. Dr. Karen thought their talks would help. David believed Jesus could help and her siblings believed if they stuck together as a family that whatever she dealt with magically disappear but they all couldn't be any more wrong. To be honest, Keisha didn't know if they would ever go away.

"Keisha, if you continue down this path of letting all of your problems consume you, you're going to find yourself in a dangerous place. That's why I'm recommending that you continue your treatment with me because I think we're right on the brink of breaking through" Karen explained and Keisha responded by laughing.

"So that's what you think? I don't feel that way at all. It seems like every page I read in this stupid diary is only making my life worse. All I'm figuring out is that I had one screwed up childhood and if my uncle would've just kept his hands to himself my life would've been somewhat normal. I probably wouldn't have even thought about being addicted to pills so if you'll excuse me Karen I think this little session we are having is officially over. I don't believe you can help me anymore" Keisha left but this time she slammed Dr. Karen's door.

When Keisha turned onto her street, she noticed David sitting on the porch using his cell phone and his truck also parked in the driveway. She didn't find his car being outside instead of in the garage odd but she couldn't understand why he sat on their front porch during the cold weather they were still experiencing. Even though the weather did steadily improve, it was still quite chilly and snowy at this time of year. She popped two pieces of sweet mint Orbit gum in her mouth and pulled in the driveway behind him.

David ended his telephone conversation just as she got out of her car.

"Hey babe, what's wrong?" Keisha inquired as she tried to read the confused expression on his face.

"Babe, do you know the electricity is off? I called the electric company and they said they haven't received last month's payment. I told them there must be a discrepancy in their system or something because I gave you the money to pay the bill..."

"I don't know what they're talkin' about," Keisha said as she looked away. She quickly tried to turn her expressions of shock to reassurance and hoped her husband brought it while she thought of how to best hand the situation.

"Babe, let me get on the phone and talk to them myself. Can you pick up the kids from school while I handle this?"

"Yeah, I'll get them. I'm going to take them over to my mom and dad's so just meet us over there after." David kissed Keisha on her cheek before pulling off in his truck. She waited until he drove down the street then dialed the electric company's number. "Hello. Yes, I would like to make a payment for 7124 Pinelake Drive."

Keisha knew the only thing she could do was come up with the money to pay the electric bill because David wouldn't take any other answer from her. She knew she should've just walked in the building and paid it like she as planned but, when she ran into Malik, she couldn't help herself. Keisha pulled out her bankcard and made a payment with her debit card. Thankfully, she was able to have a technician restore their electricity within an hour because he was already at another house nearby. She waited for them to arrive and then she took a quick shower before going over to her mother and father-in-law's house.

"I'm so glad you got that straightened around Keisha. The electric company was about to drive me insane," David said as he helped to remove her coat and hung it on the rack in the foyer of his parents' house.

"Yeah, it took me a little while but I finally got through to someone who knew what they were talking about," Keisha explained, knowing the real reason was because she failed to take care of their past due electric bill.

"Thank God!" David sighed and greeted his wife with a warm, tender kiss but the twins running from the family room interrupted their exchange.

"Hey mommy!" Katrina and D.J. yelled as if they'd rehearsed it.

She leaned down and kissed both of them on the forehead. Keisha was also pleased at her decision to take a shower and

# pretty skeletons

thoroughly brush her teeth before leaving the house. Her children didn't know of Hennessey but would've definitely sniffed out the scent like two K-9's on a drug search. Just as Keisha looked up, Cecilia joined them as she wiped her hands on her apron.

"You came just in time sweetie. I just pulled the meatloaf out of the oven." She smiled.

"Mom, you always know how to make me happy," Keisha replied as she reached out and embraced her mother-in-law, who seemed more like a mother to her than her in-law. That warmth and sweetness made her cling to the woman responsible for giving birth to the man she loved.

"And thank you for allowing us to say the night with you and dad until the morning," Keisha said as she followed her in to the dining room and helped set the table.

"It's no problem baby. That's what we're here for. Besides, we love it when our grandchildren come over."

"They love it too," Keisha said as she watched her children follow David Sr. into his office. She smiled at the sight of them with their grandfather, glad they got a chance to experience a way of life different than her own. They knew what having a mother and father was like in addition to a set of grandparents who loved them more than life itself. As far as Keisha was concerned, she wouldn't have it any other way and she didn't care what she had to do or say for them to never know about all the painful things that made up the composite of her past. Her children had a wonderful life and that's the way she wanted to keep it. She didn't have the luxury of having her father in her life. She didn't even know who he was. When she was younger she used to ask Rita where her father was and she told her father was killed shortly after she was born.

"Mom, this food smells delicious. I can't wait to eat," David announced and rubbed his stomach as they moved toward the kitchen.

"Well, don't worry. You can't eat anything until you wash your hands and make sure your father and the twins do the same," she stated.

"Yes ma'am." David answered in his little kid voice and left out the dining room.

Keisha laughed. "David is crazy, Ma, ain't he?"

"I swear my son hasn't changed one bit. Always tryin' to eat before it's time." She shook her head and sat the last dish on the table which was a large bowl of creamy cornbread mash potatoes.

"Mom, he does the same thing at our house and what's bad is he has the kids doing it too."

"It figures," she chuckled and then stopped her laughter to continue talking.

"David told me about how sick your uncle's been. I'm so sorry to hear that."

"It's okay, really. I don't know what's going on with him but I honestly don't think it's as bad as it seems."

"Well, I understand it may be hard trying to deal with that being he's partly responsible for raising you. But, I want you to know I'm here if you need me, if you ever want to talk. My door is always open." She held out her arms and hugged Keisha.

"I appreciate it, Ma. But, I'm fine."

"Okay. But just know, my offer still stands." She smiled and continued on with what she preparing the table. Keisha was satisfied with the fact her mother-in-law didn't want to press the issue any further because she didn't feel like explaining the situation to her or anybody else. All they knew was that she didn't really get along with her aunt and uncle. That was sufficient.

"Mommy, daddy told me to give you this because it's ringing," Katrina said as she handed her cell phone. Keisha covered it up with her hands and whispered.

"Who is it?"

"Daddy said Aunt Kennedi is on the phone."

Keisha sighed. "Okay, thanks baby." She placed the phone up to her ear. "Hey sis, what's up?"

"Keisha, where are you?" Kennedi asked with panic laced all throughout her tone.

"I'm at David's parents' house. What's wrong?"

"It's Uncle Jessie!"

"Kennedi, I know you're not calling me with any foolishness about Jessie 'cuz I don't want to hear it."

# pretty skeletons

"Keisha the doctors gave him three days to a week to live. We need to get there as soon as we can. It's not looking good."

"What are you saying?"

"Look, I already know how you feel about this whole situation but you need to put it all aside and come home with us. We'll be leaving in about two hours," Kennedi explained. Everything within Keisha wanted to respond curtly but she knew it was neither the time nor the place to be impious.

"Alright, I'll be ready." Keisha sighed and agreed to meet them at her house. She ended the call with the sister and stood in the middle of the dining room, trying to process what her sister told her.

"Babe, what's wrong?" David walked in and intruded her thoughts.

"That was Kennedi. She said Jessie is not doing well at all. They're giving him less than a week to live so we're going to see him."

"I want to come with you. I'll get my parents to keep the kids and we'll all drive down together," David presented.

"That's okay, baby. I know you really want to go and be there for me but this is a trip I must make alone." Keisha had mixed feeling about going to see Jessie on his death bed. She thought she would jump for joy or be happy when she knew this day arrived but odd enough she didn't feel that way. Not at all. At this point, she didn't know how to feel.

She knew she must've appeared weird to her husband for turning him away when he only wanted to come and be there with her but Keisha thought it would be better if she kept her husband out of the situation. Besides, the trip was too short to bring her husband up to speed about everything she'd never told him. The valuable information she'd previously withheld would take much longer than the distance from Akron to Columbus to explain.

# chapter 19

The entire drive to Columbus, Keisha squirmed in her seat. Her nerves had her on edge even though she managed to ingest quite a few of her problem solvers. However, they still weren't able to produce any peace as she silently regretted agreeing to see Jessie, again. Keisha highly doubted they would come to an understanding in light of his imminent death. A part of Keisha believed Jessie planned the entire hospice scenario but she doubted his ability to deceive an entire staff of health care professionals.

Alonzo pulled into the hospice facility while he talked on the phone with Darlene. Keisha's heart began to race as her brother drove up and down a few aisles trying to find a parking space. Her heart pounded with the cadence of a seasoned drummer to the point that she was afraid, if he didn't stop the madness and park soon, it would explode.

Keisha tapped him on the shoulder then pointed. "Alonzo, just park in that spot right there!" Alonzo turned his head and looked at his sister. Instead of saying something that he might regret later, he simply thanked her.

Keisha knew good and well she didn't smoke but surely felt the mood for a cigarette although she knew even that wouldn't help her calm down. So, she pulled out her cell phone and texted David.

Keisha. Hey baby, we just got here. We're about to go in now.

David. Honey my prayers are with you. I wish I could be there. I know how hard this is for you.

Keisha. Thanks. I'll text you later. Love you.

Keisha placed her phone on silent and stuffed it back inside her purse. Alonzo ended his call with Darlene and took the key out of the ignition.

"Let's go y'all. Aunt Darlene is at the entrance waiting for us."

"Hold on, let me adjust my wig," Kennedi said as she looked in the mirror and shifted her platinum blonde and burgundy hair piece.

"Kennedi, bring your dusty wig and come on," Keisha responded. She pulled the door handle and got out of the car while Kennedi smacked her super glossed up lips and fixed her last few pieces of hair.

When the automatic sliding glass doors opened, Darlene stood before them with her arms crossed. The tears she tried to hold back in attempts to be strong suddenly ran down her face freely but she mustered up enough composure to hug everyone.

"I'm so glad you're here," she said.

"Auntie. We're glad we could get here so fast. What's going on?"

Darlene rubbed her shoulders.

"I wish I knew. I mean, this all happened so fast. He was doing so much better and getting excellent reports from all his doctors and then, out of the blue, they put him back in the hospital. Now, his kidney doctor is saying he's in final stage. And, since the dialysis isn't working and there aren't any kidney donors available, they've given him a few days to a week to live." Darlene started to cry all over again. Alonzo reached out and embraced her as Kennedi stood close to them and rubbed her back.

Keisha crossed her arms, not knowing what to do or say. She lowered her head.

"What's Uncle Jessie saying about everything?" Alonzo asked as he wiped away Darlene's tears with a tissue.

"He's been in pretty much in a comatose state since he was admitted. He's awoke a few times but not for very long."

"Wow, auntie, we've been praying the entire way here and we know what the doctor's say. But, God has the final say so," Kennedi replied as Darlene shook her head.

"I know God has the power to turn it all around. I don't see Him turning this around. I've been praying God will touch my unbelief."

# pretty skeletons

Keisha was surprised to hear her aunt talk like that, especially when she'd been the spokeswoman for faith in their family. It caught her off guard to see the woman who had always been so sure of what God could do doubt His very ability.

Keisha wanted to reach out and hug her and tell her everything would be alright but she didn't want to appear fake or look rehearsed. She wanted her sympathy to be genuine, not to appear as if she wanted an Oscar. But, to be honest, she didn't really have any compassion for Jessie and his situation. The only sadness she felt was for Darlene wasting so much of her life and energy on such a low life of a person. Keisha walked in closer to her aunt and gave her a hug yet they were interrupted by a medium height, red-haired nurse.

"Darlene, I'm so sorry to interrupt you but I wanted to inform you that your husband just woke up and would like to see you."

The ambiguous expression planted on the nurse's face made it difficult to decipher if the request was a good or bad thing. But, according to Darlene's response, one would've thought he had been discharged to come home.

"Okay, we're coming right now," Darlene answered.

As they followed the nurse through the hallways, they began to absorb the tranquil atmosphere. In the lobby, a waterfall inside the wall produced a calm rhythm. Beautiful paintings also adorned the wall. The staff was very friendly and they even had a golden retriever roaming freely in the hallways, visiting from patient to patient. As they made their way toward the back of the facility, Darlene kept commenting on the peaceful and relaxing environment as well as how the staff did an excellent job making her feel at home. In the midst of their conversation, all Keisha found herself concentrating on was locating a bathroom where she could go and take a few pills. She didn't think she'd find one until they turned the last corner and a restroom sign popped up out of nowhere.

"I'll be right back. Gotta use the bathroom." Keisha made a B-line for the restroom without even looking back. She walked in and locked the door behind her. She shuffled items in her purse around until she found her bottle. She dropped four pills into her left hand and filled the palm of her right with water then swallowed them together. She knew it wouldn't be long before they kicked in and she entered into "Mellowland" but desperately hoped she'd feel the effects sooner rather than later. Keisha joined Darlene, Kennedi, and Alonzo – who waited outside Jessie's room – just as the red-haired nurse signaled for them to enter.

"Is he still awake?" Darlene asked in a hopeful tone.

"Yes. He's still up and alert. He'd like to see everyone. He told me he wasn't in any pain but, if he gets uncomfortable at all while you're here, just call for me. I'll come back and give him his scheduled PRN dose of morphine," the nurse explained.

"Okay, Janet, thank you." Darlene waited for the nurse to make her way down the hall before she said, "Come on, y'all. Let's go in."

Keisha really wanted to express to her aunt that she didn't desire to go in at all but knew she needed to put her feeling to the side. Besides, if she told Darlene she couldn't stomach looking at him, she probably would've claimed Keisha had a demon in her and tried to cast it out right here in the hallway. She concluded it was better off keeping such mean spirited thoughts to herself.

Darlene pressed on the heavy wooden door lightly until it opened, allowing them entrance into a room set up more like a bedroom than a hospital suite. They all walked in behind each other until they stood at the foot of his bed.

Jessie closed his eyes for a brief moment then opened them and smiled. "I'm so happy you could be here with me."

Everyone moved closer to Jessie except for Keisha. She remained where she felt most comfortable, at the foot of the bed.

"Keisha, why don't you move up closer too?" Jessie suggested.

"I'm fine right here." She crossed her arms and didn't bulge. Darlene glanced down at Keisha and rolled her eyes. Keisha returned the favor.

"Anyway, baby, we're just glad we could all be here with you. We're happy you're awake," Darlene smiled then looked at Keisha who picked with her nails. Her lack of attention seemed to annoy Darlene even more.

"How long have I been sleep?" Jessie asked.

Darlene looked at Alonzo before she continued. "For a while. This is the first you've been awake in three days."

Jessie pressed his lips together firmly and replied, "Wow! That's a long time!"

"Yeah, but you're up now which is a good thing." Alonzo smiled and gave him the thumbs up.

"Regardless of what the doctors say, we believe God can do anything. That's what you taught us," Kennedi added.

"Amen to that, Kennedi! And, believe me, if there's anyone who has faith it is definitely me! But, to be honest, God had given me peace about everything."

"Peace that you're going to be coming out of this?" Kennedi replied.

"Not exactly. I'm just at peace with my life. I can't really explain it but, whatever happens to me, I'm at peace because I know God's will have been done."

Jessie's religious speech was interrupted by Keisha's loud clapping. "Jessie, do you want an Oscar for that performance? Because, if it were up to me, I would be handing you the statue right now," she said as she finally moved in a little closer to the bed. She looked around at Kennedi, Alonzo, and Darlene. Their mouths dropped down to the floor as her sudden outburst shocked them but she didn't even care. She'd had enough of his ridiculous antics.

"Excuse me?" he asked with his eyebrows raised.

"Oh, now, you want to act surprised? I said would like your trophy now or after you die?"

Darlene moved from where she stood to directly in Keisha's face. "Keisha, what has gotten into you? Your uncle is on his deathbed and you don't have the decency to put all the issues you have with him to the side?"

"What's gotten into me? You need to turn your attention and ask Jessie over there what's wrong with him. I'm not the one with the problem!" Keisha crossed her arms.

"Keisha, chill! This is not the place for all this. Or, the time!" Alonzo held his hand up at his sister in attempts to stop the conversation from escalating any further but Keisha appeared to be in a trance-like state.

"Move out the way Alonzo. This is the time!"

Darlene shook her head. "I cannot believe you'd come here and start all this trouble when you know what we're going through." She sighed and continued. "And the nerve of you, too, standing here and carrying on this way after all we've done for you. You're so ungrateful!"

"Cut the thanksgiving speech, Darlene. Y'all haven't done anything for me. I may have had a place to stay for some years but it was a living hell and you know it!"

"Keisha, why are you talking to Aunt Darlene like this? If it wasn't for them, we would've had nobody," Kennedi said as she got upset.

"We provided you with the best home we could and tried to take care of you but none of that matter. Does it? You only recognize and see what you want to."

"Let me ask you this question. Was being raped and molested every night by your husband part of caring for me?" Keisha started to cry as she finally brought her eyes to look Jessie in the face. His expression was priceless, as though he'd come in contact with a Grim Reaper. However, Keisha felt like she'd literally burst if she didn't confront him.

Kennedi and Alonzo both stared at Keisha and simultaneously said, "What?"

As to follow suite, Darlene asked the same question.

"You heard me clearly. Now, answer the question!" Keisha asked as she continued to cry.

"I can't believe after all these years you're still lying about the same stuff. This is unbelievable." Darlene shook her head then turned to Jessie who still hadn't managed to say a word.

"Oh, I'm lying? So you think I've been lying about all this for all these years?" Keisha stopped talking to see what Darlene had to say.

"Honestly, I believe you've made all of this up to keep dissention in our family."

"I've made all this up, huh? Do you want to know how I'm telling the truth? Jessie has a birthmark on the inside of his groin on the left side. Now, how would I know otherwise? I wouldn't have been able to see that through any clothes. Darlene he used to come into my room and do whatever he wanted with me night after night. I didn't make that little pregnancy issue up. You made me have an abortion and I'm sorry to tell you that your precious husband over there was the father."

When Keisha finished her revelation, Darlene had been reduced to tears. Kennedi and Alonzo stood in the corner of the room, not saying anything, just looking on.

"You can stand there and act like none of these things happened but they did! They happened under your roof and even though you've called me a liar all these years, deep down inside you know I'm telling the truth!"

"Keisha, stop it! Stop it right now! I will not stand here and let you continue to lie!" Darlene scolded her.
Keisha laughed sarcastically. "Since you think I'm lying, why don't you ask him?" Keisha pointed at her uncle. "Come on Jessie! Why don't you tell her the truth?"

After he didn't respond as quickly as she thought he should, she continued. "You always have so much to say. You're pretty quiet now. Wonder why? Because, you know I'm telling the truth!"

"Okay, since you call yourself telling the truth and being honest. I bet you haven't been honest about your little drug problem you had back in the day."

He let out a devilish chuckle. "Huh? You probably never even told Alonzo and Kennedi that you fell down the same path as your mother!"

Keisha raised her hand and pointed at him.

"Look, you leave my mother out of this! I've never claimed to be perfect by any means. But, at least, I'm woman enough to admit my mistakes." Keisha replied and looked over at her brother and sister cried. The sight of them caused her tears to continue.

"Keisha, why won't you let all these false accusations go?"

"I'm not letting anything go until he confesses..." Keisha stood in silence and stared at Jessie. If looks could kill, he would be six feet under. She found it unbelievable that a man who was near the end of this life could still be in denial. She couldn't believe he still decided to keep his mouth sealed about all the things that had taken place.

"I haven't been to church in a long while but I know enough about God's word to know lying is a sin. Why can't you just tell the truth?"

There was complete silence as she continued. "For once, tell the truth. I mean, you do owe me that much. Be the so-called "Man of God" you've portrayed to be all these years and admit what you did to me, Jessie," Keisha stated as she looked him directly in his eyes.

By the solemn and worried look on Jessie's face, Keisha knew she had finally struck a nerve with him. For a while, he just laid there in silence. But, shortly after, tears started to roll down the left side of his face. He, then, reached over the nightstand and grabbed a few loose tissues be trying to compose himself enough to speak but was so overwhelmed with emotion his reply came out as a whisper.

"It's true."

Darlene turned her attention to him and asked, "Jessie, what did you say?"

He cleared his voice and spoke up, "Darlene. What she's saying, is true."

Darlene grew faint and sat down in the chair next to his bed. "Oh my God. So, what she's saying is all true?"

Jessie took a deep breath and exhaled. "Yes. Everything she's saying is true but there's more," Jessie stated as he sat up in bed and asked Darlene for his wallet. She reached inside her purse and handed a brown leather billfold to him. He opened it and went to the back of the wallet to retrieve a tattered piece of cream paper. He unfolded it and handed it to Darlene. She looked at the document over with confusion.

"I can't believe this. What is this?" Darlene asked as she read the document over one more time before speaking again.

"This is Keisha's birth certificate. Why do you have this?" Darlene inquired.

"You didn't know. Look at the line that lists her parents."
Darlene started reading. "Okay. It says Rita Sheridan is her mother and Jessie Jackson is her ... Oh my God! You're

# pretty skeletons

Keisha's father?" Darlene asked. But, from the look on Jessie's face and proof in her hands, she already had the answer.

"Yes, Darlene. I'm Keisha's father."

"Are you kidding me? And you still did what you did? Why Jessie? Why?" Keisha pleaded.

Jessie went on to explain how he had once had a relationship with Rita and they were very much in love. He even thought she was the one for him until she told him she was pregnant. He said that changed everything. And, instead of handling responsibility, it caused him to run. In the meantime, he secretly started seeing Darlene. When Rita found out, she was furious. She told him she would rather get an abortion than raise their unborn child alone. Since she'd become so angry about his new relationship with her sister, Darlene and Jessie decided to pick up and move away. He figured she'd aborted the baby but, when she contacted him through the mail about the date of her C-Section, he'd decided to be there for the delivery. After that, he had absolutely no contact with her until Rita passed and they her children were forced live with them. He also said Rita had developed a drug habit, once he left, and he believed himself to be the reason.

"You're my father? My father? That means you were supposed to protect me and you didn't," Keisha said in between tears and crossing her arms.

"I'm sorry, Keisha. But, when I first saw you, it was like staring your mother in the face. I realized I never truly gotten over her and…"

Keisha held up her hand in protest. "I think I'm about to be sick."

Keisha started walking out the room but heard Jessie continuously apologize. But, as far as she was concerned, there was nothing he could say or do to make anything better for her. He actually made everything worse. Everything Jessie admitted made her want to throw up. Honestly, she couldn't believe what she heard him say. She remembered how she always desired for him to tell the truth and admit the wrong but never imagined he would drop such a bomb on her. I guess the truth did hurt sometimes and she wished she hadn't heard him admit his mistakes because she knew more than she wanted at that point.

All Keisha desired was to take a handful of pills and forget the conversation ever occurred. She felt like a guest on some deranged episode on Jerry Springer or something. Instead this drama was her true reality and it appeared in full and living color even though she desperately wanted to erase it from her existence. However, there was nothing she could do. Her life had changed once again.

# chapter 16

"I'm ready! Let's go!" Keisha announced as she exited the women's restroom to find Alonzo and Kennedi awaiting her. She didn't even care if they responded, she walked past them and started making her way toward the exit. But, Darlene, called out to her before she got too far.

"Keisha, wait! Please wait," Darlene pleaded. Keisha stopped dead in her tracks but still didn't turn around. Her aunt quickly approached then gently grabbed her hand. Oddly enough, Keisha didn't snatch away. "Listen to me, Keisha. I had no idea that all this was going on in my house. I hope you know I would've never allowed anything like this at all!" Keisha turned around halfway to somewhat face Darlene.

"Whatever Darlene! I tried to tell you. I tried and you didn't believe me because you thought I was lying. You turned a blind eye and a deaf ear to everything I tried to tell you." A new stream of tears fell as she continued to speak. "You never even took the time out to figure out otherwise. He molested me from the time I moved in with y'all until the time I moved out. I was always made out to be the monster, but the real monster lay in your bed every night, right next to you. He's the monster and here you thought I was nothing but a trouble maker." Keisha opened up her mouth to speak but found herself too overcome with emotion.

"I am so sorry, Keisha. I should've listened to you. I don't know how I will be able to forgive myself," Darlene said as she stared Keisha in the eyes.

"I've already went through so much because of him. Now, he wants to spring on me that I'm his kid? I don't know what to tell you but all I can say is you better pray God has mercy on your soul and that man in there because the damage has already been done to me. I'm gone!" Keisha let go of her aunt's hand and walked through the exit door.

They rode on the interstate in complete silence for almost two hours. There wasn't any music paying softly in the background or conversations going on. Just complete silence. Finally, once they were almost back to Akron, Alonzo spoke up.

"Sis, I'm sorry. We had no idea any of this went on or, believe me, I would've handled it."

"I know you didn't know," Keisha replied.

"Why didn't you tell us?" Kennedi asked as she turned around in her seat.

"He threatened, on more than one occasion, to do things to you if I ever opened up my mouth to tell anyone. I was so afraid of him hurting y'all I kept quiet."

Alonzo pounded his fist against the steering wheel.

"And to think, I considered that man to be like a father. I can't believe he did that stuff to you."

"Me either," Kennedi added.

"What's done is done," Keisha replied as she leaned back in her seat and closed her eyes.

During the ride home, her mind became flooded with all the new found information. Jessie was her biological father. Not only had he molested and impregnated her, he had kept that secret her entire life. She began to think about the things that never really added up. With all of the new information, things started to fit together like pieces in a puzzle. She used to wonder why Darlene and Jessie never had anything to say when she asked questions about her father. Even though she figured her aunt didn't have a clue, Jessie sure knew and kept his mouth shut. Keisha also used to question why Darlene was never close to Rita since they were sisters. Jessie seemed to be the common denominator when it came to everything wrong with their lives. And, the thought of him being the cause made Keisha feel out of character. If she had a gun, she would drive back and end his life herself. She highly disliked him before but resolved to completely wishing him dead. Children are supposed to be able to trust and lean on parents and guardians, not be hurt by them,

## pretty skeletons

but having Rita and Jessie as parents proved that to be a very false statement.

Rita was always too high and doped up to be her mother and Jessie hadn't been able to keep his nasty hands off of her. She was already devastated by the fact she'd been sexually abused but to hear that scumbag actually confess to being her real father was the final knife twisted in her back. Why he didn't take that to his grave, she thought.

"Wake up sis, we're at your house," Kennedi said as she nudged her sister. Keisha's mind had been so active and awake with her thoughts she didn't realize she'd fallen asleep. Alonzo pulled up in her driveway and placed the car in park. He got out and walked around to help her out of the car. By the time he made it to her door, she had already got out and closed it behind her. He reached out in an attempt to hug her but she stopped him.

"Please. Don't," Keisha replied as she looked at him quickly then turned away. She sighed then started walking toward the front entrance of her house.

"I guess, I'll call you later," she replied. Kennedi called out to her. "Please call us. We love you."

"I love you too."

Keisha stuck her key in the lock and let herself in to the house. She walked through the foyer and discovered David sitting in his favorite recliner, watching ESPN.

"Hey honey. What are you doing back so soon? You guys haven't been gone for a full day," he asked as he got up and tried to greet her but she pushed him away.

"What's wrong, babe? Is everything okay?" David said as he moved in closer and tried to wrap his arms around her. She ended up stepping to the side.

"David, I really don't want to talk about it. Where are the kids?" She asked as she poked around and realized she didn't see or hear them. She started to pace back and forth.

"They are still with mom and dad. What's going on Keisha? Something doesn't seem right with you."

She didn't respond. She just continued to pace back and forth until she cried. Then, her tears caused her to become angry and she started slamming various things around the room. "David, I

185

told you! I don't wanna talk about it," Keisha exclaimed as she stared at him. She opened her purse, grabbed her car keys, and started to head toward the kitchen then to the garage door.

"Where are you going?"

"I gotta get out of here." And, as fast as Keisha had come home, she left again.

Keisha drove around the city aimlessly for what had seemed like hours as her mind raced. Even though she had no clear destination, she didn't want to be at home. She knew David must be worried sick about her but even he was the least of her concerns at this point. She began to realize the fairy tale life she had built with him was based on lies she'd fabricated because she feared how he would act toward her if he knew the truth. She figured their relationship would be thrown out the window once she exposed the skeletons hidden in her closet. She loved David with all of her heart but, since she hadn't been totally honest with him from the beginning, she doubted he would trust her after this. She figured he probably wouldn't even allow her around their children when he learned of how she'd reunited with her ugly past. She honestly could kick herself for not being open and honest with him when they first met. If she would've just opened up to him in the beginning, it wouldn't have come to this mess. The problems she dealt with because of Jessie would still exist but, at least, her husband would know the real truth about her life. There were actually times in their relationship when she wanted to come clean and tell her husband everything, leaving no details out but felt he wouldn't quite understand. He wouldn't understand the complexities that made up her life and her issues were too much to deal with for such a Godly man. She justified not being completely honest with him because she felt her children deserved to have nice peaceful life. She believed they deserved to have an upbringing her husband experienced and, by not telling him, she believed she provided that for them.

She continued to drive until she saw the low fuel button symbol pop up on her car. Keisha wasn't in the mood to stop at a gas station but knew her car would stop if she didn't get some soon. She pulled into the Shell Gas Station located on the next block and used her debit card to fill up the tank then went inside and purchased bottled water. David tried to call her phone as she was walked back to the car but she pressed the ignore button. She wasn't in the mood to talk to him.

Before she left the gas station, she emptied the remaining pills into her hand and then shoved them into her mouth. She washed them down with a swig of water and realized exactly where she needed to go.

Keisha pounded feverishly on Malik's door as she waited for him to answer.

"Malik! Open this door! I know you're home!" Keisha replied speaking to the door. Keisha took her fist and knocked even harder.

Malik flung his door open. "Keisha, why are you bangin' on my door like this? You're gonna wake my neighbors." He grabbed her arm and pulled her inside his house.

"Oh, hush your mouth! Ain't nobody gon' wake your bougie neighbors. I didn't even knock hard," Keisha said as she walked past him to the living room and plopped down on his couch.

"Please! You were knocking like you were trying to wake the dead."

"You're so sensitive," Keisha replied, taking her good old time to pronounce every word slowly.

"What brings you over my way, unannounced?" Malik asked as he checked his watch.

"Why you got company coming over or something? Get outta here," Keisha acted like she peaked around the corner. She lost her balance and fell into the wall, bumping her head. She burst into laughter.

"What's wrong with you Keisha?"

"Nothing, I'm fine. I'm chillin'....chillaxin'. I thought I would pay you a little visit, that's all."

"Then, why are your eyes all puffy?" Malik examined and tried his best to read through her upbeat attitude.

"You know what? I don't even have a clue. They've been like this all day." Keisha walked into his living room and made herself comfortable on his sofa.

"Whatever Keisha! I know you're not telling me the truth but it's cool."

187

"The truth is I just need somewhere to chill out for a while. Do you mind?"

"Naw, I don't mind Keesh. You can chill. Mi casa es su casa."

"Wow! You're speaking Spanish now?" she laughed.

"You didn't know? I'm bilingual? You better ask somebody," he replied, taking a seat at the opposite end of the couch. He reached on the coffee table and picked up the remote to turn on his sixty-two inch flat screen television.

Keisha's phone began to ring. From the tone, she knew it was David trying to reach her. "If I'm not picking up my phone, then he should get the hint I don't wanna talk," Keisha said as she pressed ignore again.

"Is that your husband?"

"Yes. I just left the house. I needed to get away and I'm not in the mood to talk to him," Keisha replied as her stomach growled.

"Apparently, you're hungry." Keisha placed her hand on her stomach. With everything that had taken place, she realized she hadn't eaten anything since she'd left for Columbus a day ago.

"Do you have anything to eat?"

"Yeah, I'll go in the kitchen and see what I can find." Malik handed her the remote and disappeared. Keisha flipped through several channels until she finally settled on Bravo. The Real Housewives of Atlanta was her favorite show and she loved when they had a marathon. She set the remote back down on the table and leaned back. She took one of the decorative pillows and placed it behind her head. She decided she'd rest while Malik found her something good to eat.

When Keisha finally woke up, wrapped up in a cashmere blanket, she realized the next day had arrived. Even though she'd slept the majority of the night away, she felt like she hadn't closed her eyes for twenty minutes yet didn't remember lying down on the couch at all. She sat up and checked the time on the cable box. It read eleven thirty.

"Good morning," Malik said as he came down the steps.

"Why didn't you wake me up?" Keisha asked with an attitude.

"You was sleeping so good, I didn't want to disturb you. So, I just put some cover over you. I figured you would get up when you were good and ready."

"Did I even eat last night?" she asked.

"Nope, not at all. I went to find you something to eat but you were out by the time I came back in here. And, your phone's been ringing like a hotline too. David's been calling, so has Alonzo and Kennedi."

"Did you answer my phone?" Keisha asked in a frenzy.

"No, I just let it ring."

"Good, 'cuz I really don't feel like talking to anyone." Keisha picked it up and saw forty-seven missed calls from David, Alonzo, Kennedi, and her boss. She knew they all must be worried sick about her but she couldn't muster up enough courage to call anyone back. She wasn't ready to talk and hoped they understood. She needed some space to process the information deposited into her memory bank the day before.

"Well, why you're ducking and dodging everyone. My phone's been blowing up too."

"Who's calling you Malik?"

"Your brother. He's frantic because no one knows where are. Before you know it, he'll be coming over here."

"Did you tell him I was here?"

"Of course not. But, I can't keep doing that. You gon' have to bounce soon. I would let you stay but you know what it is."

"Yeah, I know. I'ma get out of here. First, let me go to the bathroom." Keisha got up from the couch and put her purse on her shoulder and started moving toward the steps but Malik stopped her.

"Naw, you can use the first floor bathroom. Everything works just fine," he laughed.

"You trying to be funny?"

"Not at all. But, I don't want anything missing from my upstairs bathroom either."    "Whatever." Keisha rolled her eyes. She closed the door behind her and urinated. After she washed her hands, she checked her purse for her pill bottle which was empty. She doubled check her purse but there wasn't any spare pills that had fallen by accident. She opened the door to find Malik sitting on the steps texting someone.

"Hey, you got any more pills?" Keisha asked. She opened her leather wallet and pulled out a twenty dollar bill.

"Sorry Keisha, I'm all out. Besides, with the way you acted last night, you need to leave those things alone."

"What else you got then?" Keisha inquired. Her question caused him to look up from his phone and stare at her with the most confusing look on his face.

"What you mean, what else I got?"

"Come on Malik. You're out of pills, so I want to know what other drug you have available? I know you got something."

"I know what you asked me. But, I'm unsure of how to answer you."

"It's simple. Tell me what else you have. Heroin? You got some crack? What?"

"Hold up! Pills is one thing but that stuff you just named is a whole different world right there."

"I know. So what? What do you have?" Keisha asked again. Malik started shaking his head no.

"Keisha it really don't matter what else I have because I'm not selling it to you. Absolutely not."

"You're the compassionate drug dealer or something? It's not like I'm trying to get something off of you for free. I'm a paying customer for crying out loud."
Malik let out a frustrated sigh.

"I got some powder on me."

"Ummm, I never thought I would snort coke but I guess there's a first time for everything. How much?"

"Give me a hundred and it's yours."

Keisha reached inside of her wallet and pulled out the rest of her money. He took it from her and jogged up the steps. He returned shortly carrying a clear bag containing the white substance.

"Here you go." He handed it to her then she retreated back to the bathroom and closed the door. Keisha sprinkled the powder onto the bathroom counter and used her driver's license to separate it into lines. She remembered a few people in the past used it in front of her. It never appealed to her back then but, at that moment, Keisha would snort gasoline to help her forget about all of her problems.

She rolled up a loose dollar and inhaled her first line. She stopped midway through because it caused her nose to burn. She, then, proceeded to snort the remainder. Once she finished, she stopped and looked at herself in the mirror to wonder what had she become? She stared at the person looking back at her but somehow she didn't see herself. Had she turned into the full, fledge drug addict she vowed to never become? Yes, she started popping pills to forget about everything but all the drugs seemed to do was help her think about it even more.

She opened the door to the bathroom and turned off the light. She found Malik sitting in the same spot on the steps.

"Are you happy now, Keisha?" Malik asked.

"I'm ecstatic."

"I'm surprised you didn't need any help in there. From the way it sounded, you seem to be a pro."

"Yup. And, it's all gone." A sneaky grin creep across Keisha's face. Her answer caused Malik to practically jump out of his seat.

"What do you mean it's all gone? Please, don't tell me it's all gone," Malik said with a frantic look on his face. Keisha turned the bag upside down to serve as confirmation.

"Oh my God, Keisha! I figured you would just do a little bit. Never expected you would use the entire bag! People overdose on those amounts. That's why I didn't even want to sell you any," Malik shook his head.

"Don't worry. I'll be fine. I'm leaving now anyway. So you don't have to lie about not knowing where I am." Keisha pulled out her car keys and walked out of the house. Malik followed her.

"You really need to just go home, Keisha. For real."

She continued walking down the steps.

"Don't tell me what I need to do," she stated as she pressed the unlock button on her key chain.

"Think about your kids. You don't wanna do this to them. You don't wanna repeat the cycle.'"

Without another word, Keisha put her car in reverse and pulled out of the driveway. The last thing she wanted was to be told what to do. She especially didn't care to hear the advice coming from Malik of all people. She wished somebody would've had this lecture with her no good parents so she wouldn't have been in this predicament.

As she drove, Keisha began to think about her messed up life. Why couldn't she just have a normal one like everyone else? Why couldn't she have grown up like her husband or how her children were currently being raised?

She had always played the cards life dealt to her but had to admit it was indeed a bad hand.

The more she drove, she felt herself finally start to relax and she seemed relieved. She started to feel light and carefree while all of the thoughts trying to consume her mind appeared to float away. Keisha listened to Floetry's "Say Yes" and felt as mellow as the melodic song resonating through her speakers. She was determined to not let anything destroy this feeling she experienced. She felt better than she did when popping pills and didn't want the euphoria to end. Keisha became so laid back she didn't realize she'd drove straight through a pothole until it was too late. She tried to continue until her car would no longer move.

"I swear this is not happening," Keisha put her car in park and turned the CD player down. She pulled out her cell phone to call for roadside assistance but realized it was completely dead so she threw it onto the passenger's seat.

She got out of her car, locked her doors, and started to walk to the nearest business. She noticed her vision becoming blurry and her head dizzy as she continued down the street. Keisha hoped to reach a phone soon because she honestly felt faint. When she was halfway down the road, she heard a familiar voice call out to her.

"Keisha? Is that you?" a woman asked. She immediately knew it was Dr. Karen. Sure enough, she drove beside Keisha in her navy blue Toyota Avalon.

"I'm fine," she said as she continued to walk away slowly.

"Why are you walking? Do you need a ride?"
Keisha turned her head slightly and shook her head no.

"I don't need a ride," Keisha stumbled but recovered in enough time so she didn't fall. "I'm cool, Karen."

## pretty skeletons

"You're stumbling. Are you sure you're okay?" Karen shouted. She stopped her car and got out.

"Yeah! I'm fine," Keisha slurred. But, just as Dr. Karen approached her, Keisha fainted.

# chapter 17

**W**hen Keisha came to herself, she realized she was lying in a hospital bed with numerous machines hooked up to her body. She noticed there were two I.V. lines attached to her right arm while her natural reaction was to jump up but she literally couldn't move. She felt like her body had been run over by a semi. Her eyes scanned the circumference of the room and the bed next to her appeared untouched. Her husband sat next to her, asleep in a leather recliner. Keisha gathered the little strength she possessed and touched him on the shoulder.

"Baby..." she grunted. "Wake up. Baby, what's going on?" Keisha slowly asked then paused to allow him some time to respond. It took him a moment but finally he yawned and wiped his eyes. As soon as David saw Keisha awake and speaking, he jumped up.

"Oh my God! You're awake! Thank God!" David leaned in and kissed Keisha on her forehead.

"How did I get here?" she questioned with a confused look on her face.

"Babe, you passed out and some lady was there to call an ambulance," he explained as he smoothed a piece of unruly hair out of her face. Keisha heard her husband continue telling her how she landed in the hospital but everything in her mind seemed to be all blur together into one big mess. She thought about what he said but nothing made sense to her. She lay there for a few minutes taking things in and then it was as if a light bulb went off because memories of what happened started rolling in like flooding waters. She started to remember her driving through a pot hole and getting a flat tire, seeing Dr. Karen, and even fainting. Things started to become clearer with each passing minute.

"I don't really know anything else but the lady that called 911 was nice enough to follow behind you in the ambulance to make sure everything was okay," David explained. Keisha let out a long sigh and then yawned.

"How long have I been here?"

"Four days."

"Wow!" Keisha replied and tried to fold her hands in her lap. She felt so ashamed to be up in some hospital bed because of a drug overdose and even more ashamed her husband didn't have an idea why.

"Where is everyone else at?"

"Well, I sent Alonzo and Kennedi home for a while. We've been sitting with you in shifts. Mom and dad have the kids but mom is on her way up here as we speak."

By then, a nurse entered the room and immediately began to examine Keisha. Pleased with her recovery, she allowed the couple to resume their conversation.

Keisha went to open up her mouth and say something else but David beat her to it.

"I'm so glad that you're finally awake. God definitely answers prayers. I never stopped believing He would touch your body. I also feel like it's the perfect time to talk about all that has happened."

She felt as though he'd stolen the words right out of her mouth and knew that it was finally time to come clean, about everything. The entire time they talked, she knew he would eventually want to know but she was unsure of how to proceed.

# pretty skeletons

"I agree. We definitely need to do that." Keisha stated. She paused momentarily to shift herself into an upright position just as a light knock rapped at the large wooden door. David got up from his chair and opened it. When Cecilia looked past her son and saw Keisha sitting up in bed, a huge smile appeared on her face. She walked over to her and kissed her on the cheek.

"Ma, can you give Keisha and I a few minutes. We have to talk about some things."

Cecilia moved to turn around and walk out of the room but Keisha stopped her.

"Ma, please stay. You need to hear what I have to say as well." Keisha took another deep breath, closed her eyes, and continued.

"I know, in these past few days, you've probably heard or discovered a lot of things about me that doesn't even sound right and I realize I must come clean about my past in order to move on." Keisha closed her eyes and tried to stop her tears from falling. It was already too late. A few had escaped. David didn't say anything. He grabbed some tissues off of the nightstand beside him and handed them to her.

Keisha folded her piece of tissue in half, clutched it in her hand, and started talking until she laid every bone out on the table. A new supply of tears collected in Keisha's eyes as she thought about all she admitted. She became choked up with emotions as if a noose around her neck threatened to drain the very life from her body. She could barely speak and, when Keisha looked into David's eyes and continued to cry, he started to cry right along with her.

"I was wrong for keeping this from you but I never really told anyone until now."

"Why did you wait so long to tell me these things, Keisha?"

"I was scared, honestly. I didn't know how you would react. Didn't think you would want to be with me. Look, I understand if this is all too much for you to handle but I can't hold it in any longer."

"Keisha, why would you ever think I'd leave you because of your past?"

"We came from two completely different walks of life. Why would you stay with someone like me?" Keisha asked then awaited his response. She had always known her husband to be an understanding and loving but figured there was only so much one person can take. Maybe he was at his personal breaking point, she thought, and would choose not to stay with her.

David joined hands with her and offered a slight smile. "Honey, when I said those vows to become your husband, I meant every single word. I'm not leaving you and you can count on that. I love you."

"I love you too but I just feel like the entire life we've built together is all a lie. Everything I've portrayed to be was false and I feel so low."

"Don't feel that way. You and I have such a great life together. We have wonderful children and the things you've experienced in your past mostly were not your fault. I believe you dealt with things the best way you knew how. Please don't blame yourself." David leaned in closer, sat down on the bed, and wrapped his arms around her.

"I'm so sorry, baby," Keisha said barely above a whisper.

"I'm sorry too. I'm sorry you had to go through all of this."

# pretty skeletons

"Keisha, my son is right. Regardless of what happened in the past you can't continue to beat yourself up. The important thing is you're still here and that's what matters most."

Keisha looked at her mother-in-law, who stood beside her, with tears in her eyes.

"I know mom but it still feels like I let my entire family down."

"Honey believe me, you haven't let us down at all. My husband and I are blessed to have you as a daughter. I always prayed to the Lord and asked Him to give me a daughter and that's exactly what he did. We all have issues we need to work on but just because we have them don't make us bad people. It just makes us that more real. I want you to know we love you and we're standing with you through it all." Keisha reached out and hugged Cecilia.

"I love you too and thank you."

"There's one more thing I want to say to you," David spoke. "Now, I know you've had your own personal reasons in the past for not trusting and believing in God but today's a new day and, since you've been blessed to have another chance, I hope you will in turn give God another chance."

Keisha continued to cry as David and his mother joined hands. Out of all the years she'd attended church and heard various pastors and ministers speak about God, she'd never remembered God to be presented in such a plain and simple manner. She had spent her entire life running from so many things but figured it was finally time to stop. She wiped her eyes with the last piece of tissue and then she shook her up and down.

"Mom, I'm ready to give Him another chance."

Cecilia closed her eyes and started praying right there in the hospital room. At first, Keisha kept her eyes somewhat open. She looked on at her mother-in-law as she prayed hard, sounding as if she prayed heaven down to earth. When she approached the throne of grace on Keisha's behalf, Keisha couldn't stop crying. Her tears turned into sobs. She felt every weight and burden she'd carried around for so many years being lifted out of her body. It felt good to release all of the hurt and anger that had been a part of her life for so long.

"And, we ask all these things in Jesus name. Amen." Cecilia ended the prayer then pointed upward toward the ceiling. "You give Him all of your pain and watch him take care of it. He'll do it, honey," she continued. She kissed Keisha, gave them both a hug and put on her brown leather jacket.

"Thank you for praying for me. I never thought I would say this but it was just what I needed."

"You're welcome. Let me get back to these kids. I promised them I would bring them some McDonald's when I came home." She smiled while her statement caused laughter to erupt between them all.

"Only our kids. They think they're so slick. Please don't fall into their traps," Keisha allowed a chuckle escape from her mouth.

"I believe it's too late. Your dad and I have already fallen." Cecilia laughed and grabbed her keys from her coat pocket. She walked to the door and pulled it open.

"Make sure you kiss my babies for me."

Once Cecilia left, Keisha decided to take a nap and get some rest. When she woke up, she saw David sitting in the same chair he'd been in earlier but watching some football game on ESPN.

# pretty skeletons

"Hey babe, how long was I sleep?" Keisha yawned and wiped her eyes. David glanced down at his black and silver Movado watch.

"About an hour."

"I thought by now you would've surely been gone."

"Gone where?"

"To the barbershop. I know you still have clients today, right?"

"Babe, I don't care about the shop right now. I've been right here since you were admitted. My business is important but not more important than you."

"Aww honey, what did I ever do to deserve you?" Keisha kissed him softly on his lips.

"My question to you is, what have I done to be blessed with a beautiful woman like you. God must really love me."

Keisha's phone vibrated on the night stand. She motioned for David to hand her the phone. She had two voicemail messages so she pressed the button to listen. The first message was from the detective assigned to her brother's case. She increased the volume on her phone.

I've been trying to call you and your brother for the past few days to inform you that we've had a sudden break in the case. I would like to speak with you soon. When you get this message, please give me a call back. Talk to you soon.

Keisha felt so relieved that the detectives made some progress, grateful they were still trying to find out who was responsible for beating Alonzo especially when many cases go unsolved. She decided she would give him a call later on that evening.

Her next voicemail message began to play immediately after the previous one. It was from Darlene.

Keisha. I know I'm the last person you probably want to hear from right now but I heard about what happened to you and I'm on the way to the hospital as we speak. I should be there shortly. Bye.

Keisha pressed the end button on her phone and handed it back to David. He looked at the weird expression on her face and became concerned. "Babe, who was that?"

Keisha explained.

"Babe, I'll stop her at the door if that's what you want me to do. I won't allow her to come in here and upset you," David offered. But, suddenly there was a change in Keisha's countenance. She replied.

"It's okay. She's another person I really need to talk to."

Keisha knew they needed to have a real conversation without all of the arguing and bickering back and forth. She just prayed she would be able to do so in such a short amount of time.

# chapter 18

"**S**is, it's so good to see you up and about," Kennedi said as she walked through the door and saw Keisha coming out of the bathroom in a gray jogging suit. Keisha looked at her sister and began to laugh.

"Oh my gosh! Just when I think it can't get any worse. Can you please explain to me why you have pink and black hair up in your head?" Keisha sat on the hospital bed and began to brush her hair into a neat ponytail.

"Keesh, now you know my hair is fly. And it even matches what I have on today. To top it all off, I have on my new pair of Coach shoes that Quincy brought me." Kennedi turned around in a circle and walked halfway across the room to showcase her outfit.

"I hope you guys are saving money instead of spending it all especially when you don't know when he'll find a job." Kennedi's face lit up as soon as she heard her sister mention the word job.

"Oh, I'm pleased to announce he just got hired back at his old job and is making close to eighteen dollars an hour so we're no longer at odds with each other. Everything is all good in my household." Kennedi smiled from ear to ear. Keisha, glad to hear that piece of information, honestly hoped Quincy could hold on to such a good job instead of quitting. Kennedi really needed him to step up to the plate and take care of his responsibilities so everything seemed to be falling into place for her.

"Sounds good, sis. Where's Alonzo?"

"Oh, he's parking the car right now. He said he has something to tell us but wants to wait until we're all together."

"Okay. That's cool. Babe, are you hungry? Why don't you go down to the cafeteria and grab something. You've been here with me all day, go and take a break," Keisha encouraged David.

"Are you sure? I can stay if you need me to."

"No, I'll be okay honey. Why don't you go home and get yourself cleaned up and then come back."

"I think I'll do that. Thanks babe. If you need anything, please call me. I'll be back up here after a while." David leaned over, kissed Keisha, and left.

Kennedi waited until David closed the door before she spoke. "I'm so glad you sent him home. I don't think he's been since you came in here. So how are you feeling?"

"I'm feeling good. The doctors are going to let me go home tomorrow. Everything is looking fine."

"That's great. We were all praying for you."

"I know you were and I really appreciate it," Keisha replied and gave her a hug. Alonzo came in and interrupted their sisterly moment.

"Break all of this mushy gushy stuff up. And you better not ask me to come and join in because I'm not." Alonzo took off his coat and acted like the sight of them hugging each other made him sick.

"Oh whatever, bro. Stop acting like that." Keisha laughed.

"I'm just playing. I'm so happy to see you awake."

"So what did you have to tell us, Zoe? Inquiring minds want to know," Kennedi said as he took his seat in the chair David previously occupied.

"I got a chance to speak with Detective Parker and they've finally found the person responsible for assaulting me."

"Okay, who is it? Somebody we know?" Keisha asked. Alonzo paused and then looked at both of them before he spoke again.

"Malik."

"Are you serious? How did they find that out?" Keisha asked as her mouth dropped to the ground.

"Well, one of his neighbors reported him to the police due to suspicious activity. When they obtained a search warrant and went through the house, they not only found enough drugs to put him away for the rest of his life, they also found items suggesting he was the one responsible for my assault."

"Wow. What did they find?" Kennedi inquired.

"Tapes with phone conversations, emails between Malik and the men who actually attacked me, and even a letter he'd written explaining how he would pay them once they completed the job."

"So you're trying to say Malik set you up?" Keisha raised her eyebrows as she tried to process all the information Alonzo just told her while thinking about her own encounters with Malik and his intentions where she was concerned.

"Exactly. He tried to set me up and hoped those guys beat me up so bad I would've succumbed to my injuries."

"I can't believe him. Why would he do something like that?" Kennedi crossed her arms. Her nostrils began to flare as she waited for Alonzo to answer her question.

"Apparently, when we both got in trouble back in the day, he felt like I should've gone to prison right along with him. But, since I didn't have a previous record, I got to go free. Ever since then, he's felt as though I needed to pay for the things he had to go through and has been planning on finding a way to seek revenge."

"That's so messed up. So, is he in jail right now?"

"Yeah. And, from all of the charges they've slapped him with, he won't be getting out in our lifetime and I'm glad."

"I know you must feel crazy that your so called best friend did all this to you."

Alonzo sighed and rubbed his face.

"Yeah, man it's crazy how the one person you trust to be your best friend, with your very life, is the very same person that's trying to take you out. But, all I can say is I'm glad he's in prison where he belongs."

Keisha shook her head back and forth. She never imagined in a million years that Malik would do something like that to her brother, especially since he claimed they were so close they should be blood. I guess his portrayal of such a close friend to Alonzo was just a front so he could stay close enough to get him back. She was glad that his plans didn't succeed. People like Malik were only loyal to one person, themselves.

# JESSICA A. ROBINSON

There was a light knock at the door and the nurse who had been caring for Keisha all day walked in. "I was coming to see if you needed anything. Also, you have a visitor that's here to see you as well."

"No, I don't need anything. I'm fine. But who's here?"

"She said her name's Darlene. She would like to speak with you but wanted me to ask first," the brunette haired nurse asked.

"Yeah, that's fine. She can come in." Keisha replied without even blinking an eye. The nurse turned around and walked in the direction of the door.

"Okay, I'll go to the waiting room and get her."

"Sis, are you sure you want to see Aunt Darlene? I know her and Uncle Jessie really upset you the last time we were all together," Kennedi said as she stood up next to the bed.

"Yeah, I'm sure I want to see her. Besides, I think it's time we talk. For real this time."

"Okay, do you want us to step out?"

"That would be a good idea."

Just as Kennedi and Alonzo walked out of the room, Darlene entered and stood near the door.

"Hey Keisha. I tried to get down here as soon as I could. I'm sorry to hear about what happened." Darlene said as she continued to stand in the same spot.

"You can come in and sit down if you want."

Darlene accepted the invitation. She removed her suede black coat and matching gloves and smoothed her chin length hair back in place.

"I know that I'm one of the last people you want to see right now but I wanted to come in person and talk to you. Kennedi called me this morning and told me that you were finally awake. I told Jessie I needed to get up here."

"Jessie's still alive?"

"Yeah, he's still alive and out of the hospital. He's actually here with me but I told him to stay in the waiting area. I didn't want him to cause you any aggravation."

God performed a miracle in Jessie's life and allowed him to live, Keisha thought. The last time she'd seen him, he had been given only a few days to a week to live. She figured God spared

206

him once again for a reason and didn't admit it but she was amazed. Keisha still hadn't said anything to Darlene because she was waiting for the right words. To be honest, she had disrespected Darlene for so many years that she wasn't exactly sure of how to approach her. All she could think to do was pray, Lord... please help me. Help me to say what needs to be said. Keisha went to open her mouth to start talking but Darlene interrupted her. "Look, Keisha, before you say anything please just hear me out. I want to apologize to you for how everything went down over the years. When you came to me and told me all those things about Jessie, I should've believed you because you were just a child but I chose to believe a man over my own flesh and blood. That was wrong. I should've investigated your accusations but, instead, I decided to ignore them like they didn't exist and I'm sorry. I'm sorry for all of the pain you had to go through and I should've been there for you. I am your blood and I wasn't there for you. You had to go through all of those horrible things. And, when you came to me and brought it to my attention, I called you a liar. I did the same thing to you that your grandmother did to me and your mother," Darlene said with tears beginning to pool in her eyes.

Keisha couldn't stop her tears from falling either and wasn't the least bit surprised because that's all she had been doing lately.

"What are you talking about?"

"When your mother and I were little, we were in a similar situation. Instead, the guy molesting us was our mother's friend who used to watch us while she was at work. We tried telling her but she didn't believe us. Our mother went to her grave still believing her daughters were nothing but little liars. I promised myself that I would do my best to prevent anyone else from going through the same pain and I allowed the same thing to happen to you. I'm sorry Keisha. If you can find it in your heart to forgive me that's all I want. If you can't, I understand." Darlene buried her face in her hands and continued to weep. Keisha could tell her aunt was truly sincere and her apology was straight from her heart.

"Aunt Darlene, I want you to know that since I've been in the hospital I've been doing a lot of thinking and I do forgive you. All this time, I thought I would tell you off or say some things to hurt your feelings because I wanted you to feel like I did but I don't feel that way anymore. I forgive you and I forgive Jessie. What happened was messed up but I can either choose to remain shackled to my past or live life and truly move on. That's what I plan to go forward."

Keisha wiped away her tears and continued. "I realized that, by hating you and holding spite in my heart, I wasn't hurting you at all. I did more damage to myself. I don't want to live like that anymore so I forgive you, not for just you but also for me. With my life almost slipping away like it did, I know it isn't promised and I might not have another chance to make amends so I feel this wouldn't be right if Jessie is not here to hear this too."

Darlene left out the room. Shortly after, returned with Jessie and Keisha didn't waste any more time beating around the bush.

"Jessie, since I've been hospitalized, I've given my life over to Christ. I want you to know I forgive you. I know we've had our differences over the years but that's all a thing of the past. I'm choosing to move on, to forgive everything you've done to me."

As Keisha finished speaking, she noticed Darlene and Jessie were both crying. She never expected her words or what she said to even touch them the way it did but she figured God works in mysterious ways.

"Keisha, I was up in that hospital bed hanging on for dear life and I prayed and asked God to give me another chance. I told the Lord, if He gave me another chance at my life, I would come and make things right so I ask you to forgive me for everything I've ever done to you. All of the secrets I've kept from you and all of the pain I've caused. I'm so sorry. That's why God has given me this opportunity to admit I was wrong and asked for your forgiveness. I realized I kept you in your own personal prison because of the things I did to you and it wasn't your fault. So, from the bottom of my heart, I ask you to forgive me," Jessie explained as his tears fell onto his shirt making their own design.

# pretty skeletons

To their surprise, Keisha held out her arms and motioned for him to come closer to her.

"You're forgiven."

# chapter 19

(Epilogue)

## 1 year later

Keisha paced back and forth in one of the green rooms located back stage at New Word Christian Center. She had recently celebrated one year of sobriety and was asked by the women's fellowship to share her personal testimony during their conference. She tried sitting down on the black plush leather couch situated in the back of the comfortable room but that didn't help so she walked the perimeter with her cream Jimmy Choo heels making their own indentation in the taupe Berber carpet.

She breathed in and out and deeply exhaled as she tried to calm her nerves but, as each minute passed, she found herself growing more and more anxious. Part of her was nervous because, other than family, she had never really told anyone else what she'd been through. Plus, she'd never spoken in front of an audience. Thank God there was a mirror nearby because she practiced the beginning of her testimony until she memorized it by heart. Occasionally, she checked her hair which was styled neatly into a bun with a side swept bang. Keisha bowed her head and said a silent prayer but a knock at the door interrupted her.

"Are you ready?" Cecilia asked, as she walked in with a huge smile on her face. Keisha took a deep breath and replied, "I'm ready as I'll ever be."

"Well, the first lady sent me on a mission to bring you out because they are ready but, before we leave, I want you to know

I'm proud of you. I know you're nervous but God is with you. Take your time and let the Lord use you. Your story will help so many women who've been through the exact same thing." Cecilia hugged Keisha and then walked her down the hallway and into the sanctuary and onto the stage. There was a brief introduction given by Cecilia then she handed Keisha a cordless mic.

Keisha took another deep breath. As she looked out in the crowd, she spotted Ms. Gina, Dr. Karen Stone, Darlene, and her sister Kennedi out in the crowd and ready to cheer her on. She pressed her lips together and smiled at them briefly before she spoke.

"First, I would like to give all honor and praise to God who is truly the head of my life. Our wonderful pastor and first lady for allowing me to come forward and tell my testimony. I count it such an honor to stand before you and tell you all of the wonderful things God has done for me. But, in order for me to declare His blessings, I have to tell you the things I've gone through," she said then took a deep breathe.

"I never thought I would be able to stand before you and reveal the things I've went through because, to me, my past represented such a very dark place in my life but I realized that was nothing but a trick of the enemy to have me think that if I remain silent then everything would be okay. But, I'm not in captivity anymore. I'm a free woman today."

"Amen. Take your time, honey," a woman shouted.

"By the age of sixteen, I had lost my mother to a drug overdose, been molested, and became pregnant with my father's child. I was addicted to drugs," Keisha continued.

"I know that's more than some people go through in a lifetime but that was my life. Many people would've lost their minds behind what I went through but thanks to God and the people he has placed before me, He has truly kept me. For so many years, I ran. I ran from the ones I felt hurt me. I ran from all of the pain, the hurt that I had inside. I thought if I could just ignore the fact that these things happened then they would all go away. But, that wasn't the case. I used to wish I could erase all of the anger I felt inside but, no matter what, the personal anguish and torment remained. However, through a series of events, I was forced to go back in time and deal with every single issue I ever had tried hide. I was forced to peel away the makeup, the perfect hair, the fairy tale family that I had worked so hard to create to deal with the real monster behind it all. Me. Through my personal journey to my healing, I realized I had to go back and confront the skeletons in my closet because they were the very things that handicapped me. Exploring those issues have been very difficult but they were necessary in order for me to move on. For so many years, I played oblivious to the fact they still existed and, even though my outward appearance appeared to be absolutely perfect, that didn't destroy their ugly presence in the background of my life. It wasn't until I landed in the hospital over a year ago from a drug overdose that I realized it was time for me to wake up. I knew I needed to get myself together and start my life over. I admitted myself into a rehab program, got clean, and started anew. In that time, I also gave the problems and issues I dealt with to Christ because He's the reason why I'm still alive. And, even though I had previous issues with God, I had to let it all go.

I also had to forgive the people in my life who I felt did me wrong. And it wasn't easy at all but I had to in order to truly be done with everything. When you choose to forgive someone, it's not for them. It's for you. There is no way I would be able make any progress in my life if I didn't choose to walk in forgiveness. I've been truly set free from all of the ugly things that have plagued me for years, and I thank God. I used to be sort of an atheist. I didn't even believe in God and wasn't interested in getting to know anything about Him at all. But He is the one who orchestrated all of these events to make me recognize my need for Him. I may have messed up along the way but I'm a prime example of God being the God of a second chance. And while I've ran mostly my entire life from everything, I'm happy to confess that I'm not running anymore."

Keisha ended her testimony and handed the microphone back to the mistress of ceremony. As she walked down the aisle to where her family sat, the congregation were all on their feet clapping their hands and crying tears of joy. She was glad that her testimony was received so well by the church. She never pictured herself to be in this place in her life.

Free as a bird.

Free from every single thing that had her shackled.

This feeling of freedom was all new to her but she was determined to do what she had to do to remain in that place because freedom never felt so good.

# pretty skeletons
# Discussion Questions

1. Do you think the absence of a mother plays a significant role in how a child deals with things in the world?
2. Keisha sought therapy throughout the course of the book. Do you agree or disagree with this method of dealing with issues? Why or why not?
3. Do you feel Dr. Karen overstepped her boundaries as Keisha's therapist? If so, why do you feel this way?
4. Discuss the reasons why Keisha didn't believe in God. Were her reservations about God and Christianity valid? Why or why not?
5. Do you feel Keisha should've harbored ill feelings toward her Aunt Darlene?
6. Do you think Keisha was wrong for not being honest with her family and her spouse about her past?
7. In the story, Keisha's addiction to prescription pills is introduced. Do you feel this is a true drug addiction? If so, discuss reasons why people self-medicate.
8. If you were Keisha could you forgive Jessie?

# about the author

JESSICA A. ROBINSON is a fresh, new author from Ohio. She's also one-fourth of a national Hip-Hop group named Carnival who released their sophomore CD in 2009. She has always been an avid reader but came into the wonderful world of writing by accident. Upon losing her father when she was ten to pancreatic cancer, she began journaling as a form of therapy. The emotions and thoughts expressed on paper turned into short stories and continued to evolve from there.

# JESSICA A. ROBINSON

Coming from such a rich background in the church of having twelve ministers in her family, she writes about the things she's went through and the things people have gone through around her. Her spiritual heritage was the breeding ground for her very own genre, "Church Dramedy."

# pretty skeletons

## Ordering Information

Yes! Please send me _____ copies of
Jessica A. Robinson's,
*Pretty Skeletons.*

Please include $15.00 plus $4.00
shipping/handling for the first book and $1.00
for each additional book.

<u>**Send my book(s) to:**</u>
Name:_____
Address:_____
City, State,
Zip:_____
Telephone:_____
Email:_____

Would you like to receive emails from
Peace In The Storm Publishing?
____Yes                    ____No

Peace In The Storm Publishing, LLC.
Attn: Book Orders
P.O. Box 1152
Pocono Summit, PA 18346
www.PeaceInTheStormPublishing.com